Half Moon Waking

Rising, Falling, and Walking through Marriage, Motherhood, and Miscarriage

by Liv Hunziker

PAGE OF NOTES
BERN CANTON, SWITZERLAND

QUALITY CONTROL AND E-BOOK CONSULTING
Jessica Powers of Catalyst Press, jlpowers@evaporites.com, jlpowers.net
BOOK DESIGN
Kathy McInnis, kathy@ivyleafdesigns.net

Dedicated to Walter, Mom, and Dad . . .

Without you three, this book would not exist.

I love you.

Whether through impossible times or times of ease,
EXISTENCE *itself is, I believe, an incredibly beautiful gift.*

Special thanks to Jesus Christ, for giving me existence
and for trusting me with this book assignment.

GLORIA DEO

ÄRA TILL GUD

Praise for *Half Moon Waking*

*From cosmic dust entering our atmosphere, to breastfeeding, to say nothing of
the author's doubts and thoughts about the mysterious workings of God:
Half Moon Waking sends us in all directions. Liv Hunziker's poetry ranges far and wide,
while her fiction introduces us to characters next door whom she allows to speak for themselves.
Grab a good cup of tea and take out your earplugs.
This volume is worth a read!*

—DAVID HORN,
author of *Soulmates* and *Return to the Parish.*

*Half Moon Waking explores the journey of motherhood as a hiker explores a new trail.
Stopping quietly along the side of life's road, Liv beautifully fastens words together in essays,
fiction, and poetry to show what is gained and what is lost in being a parent.*

—LINDA F. LEIN, M.F.A.,
is mother of two adult sons, and has authored four books,
including *Hannah Kempfer: An Immigrant Girl.*

*Yes, it is possible; we can hold the broken in one hand, grace and beauty in the other.
Liv's nature poems illustrate exactly how this can be done.
Whether in marrying, parenting, or miscarrying—here in this collection
we find a writer who understands. And cares. Her essays and fiction compassionately
illuminate usual and unusual aspects of mothering—carrying life, holding miscarriage,
enduring arduous physical and emotional labor, letting go, and especially,
learning to smile through uncertainty. The moment we enter* Half Moon Waking
*(like stepping into a shadowy barn), we'll face the damp, breathing questions
which Liv has already nurtured into existence.*

—Born in Seoul, KIMYIBO
studied art and printmaking at University of
Pennsylvania and Seoul National University.
KimyiBo lives with her husband and two children
in Berlin and Los Angeles. kimyibo.com

"Do not be angry with the rain;

it simply does not know how to fall upwards."

—VLADIMIR NABOKOV—

TABLE OF CONTENTS

Her mind is closed for this moment about to take her higher.

Meekness

the hardened, grey back
of Leviathan rose up
out of our deep and cool pools of remaining bitterness

cheerful waves forgot blue, forgot gold
as white and turquoise
and you and I rose high and slapped
dangerously
each other

Our little castle in the fast sand was out of mind.

     still   still
   with thirst and brown sand
     our Moby Dick resurrection
  will bring us today to the whole earth

  and new slivers of silver rusted harmony

       blue skies tomorrow
       will still hold Empyrean palaces of clear   for us

Manure and Reviving Eden

i find my own path to channel elated breath
into a dark horse stall on a summer morning

gold straw wisps   and sisters   strong strands   hope with and hope for

something kind?
sometimes
a summer ain't sweet

sweat haunts with the ache that heals   there is joy in the pain
while we exist
soft
quiet
attacks   hurt
we all escape words
hay   urine   grain   yellow   blend together like concrete   endorphins floating young
manure stirring the sticks of straw

muscles lifting have a way   to excite living and a fist around our purpose
methane   ammonia   carbon dioxide   insisting to stay in my nostrils and throat fifty-five years more

we must learn to love the dark and leave old hopes   paradise   and old lights
in the past

brown   summer-faded   muck   fiercely tied to the stall floor with strongest air
something about hay and dirt underfoot does so good to the base of the heart

a barn welcoming and recycling a rare sunray
with shadowed   yet new anticipation
what was supportive   what was real
willing connection or willing decay   stark bonding or
instead as dry oats

forward heaves the eight-prong pitchfork
hoist   straw   push   wet   tip   load
guide the wheelbarrow
to a fresh breeze in pastures of awake green where a new light sits

and

outside the horse-home-pen
dump it all

The Truth about Current Events;

and the Truth about Real Love

Our beautiful dust dancing.
It escapes the borders of hay,
alfalfa, race,
Syria and winter's damp.
The history lies in barns.

A FICTION STORY

A new school year came around. New kindergartners stood with their moms near the bus stop. New seniors replaced the old, at the back of my bus.

I leaned forward, cranking the large lever to open the sliding door while peering at the kindergartner. She stared at me, and I could literally see the child gulp. Big lump in her teeny neck. And then her mom said, "Okay, you need to step on now. You could sit by that girl wearing the earrings—in the front seat? I love you." Her mother's palm and fingers nearly covered the girl's entire back as she was nudged forward.

I smiled at the new passenger and waited for her to shuffle toward an open seat. We all heard a broad roar as I pressed the great machine into motion again.

I could have driven this route through Alexandria with my eyes closed. I'd been at it nearly thirty years, still found it rewarding.

Autumn meant corn for dinner at our Bruker family home that evening. Prairie grasses in the meadow across the county highway began losing their summer-green sheen. Peaceful. Ellie and I were a tad chilly, but enjoyed the evening air as we climbed onto our picnic table bench. My Esther was experiencing her first day of classes at Macalester College, so her presence was noticeably missing at our picnic.

"Well, I'm glad we can still eat outside," I said to Ellie. "Not too cold yet."

"Yeah, isn't that nice?" Ellie hastily and forcefully pressed the ceramic corn dish onto a hot pad, then distractedly scratched an itch, which actually didn't exist, on her right cheek. "—Jason, we're eating now!"

My boy, twenty-five-year-old Jason, shuffled into the yard, wearing socks. He had that groggy look he always had after watching hours of the sports channel. He had never played on a team, but his eyes were frequently glued to the Wild, Vikings, or an NBA game.

He heaved himself over the picnic bench and stared at his plate.

"Well, here we are!" Ellie tried to foster a cheery climate as she sat down. "You start the corn, Jim," she instructed. I started the corn.

I could hear the cars rushing by on the highway behind us. We're pretty lucky to have a house in the country. A little yellow house with a basement, near County Road 61. Jason kind of took over the basement, but that was fine.

"How was work, Jim?" Ellie's shoulder-length brown hair looked warm and full in the light of the setting sun and seemed to protect her from the autumn air like a scarf. She still had on the red blouse and black slacks she'd worn to work. She taught English at the high school. We both dressed up fairly nice for work. Part of doing our jobs well.

"Fine, thanks."

She flashed a grin, and my heart sped up. Just grateful. It is a real treasure when someone can care enough to genuinely smile at hearing that I had a good day.

Jason was busy with his corn on the cob. I saw him, from my side vision, in the same way that I saw the setting sun over his left shoulder.

"Jim, I think Jason needs the butter."

"Here you go, sir. Did you work today?"

Jason shook his head.

"Jim, you have corn in your teeth." I worked the corn out with my tongue.

More cars whizzed by.

"Well, I wonder how Esther is doing?" Ellie said.

"Yeah. Probably settling in, figuring things out."

"Our first child out of the house."

"Yeah . . . . We have some new drivers this year. Young ones. Esther's age. I wonder how they'll do, come winter. Bet they'll be slipping and sliding."

"I'm sure they'll be fine, Jim."

I noticed the setting sun, only its final sliver, bright gold.

I was sitting at the middle school parking lot the next morning, dropping off junior highers and waiting for the elementary kids to change buses before I would make my Cleveland, McKinley, and Adams school stops. A brown-haired girl, with a bouncing step and thick, bobbed hair pranced by my open door, with a sixth-grade boy on each side of her. "You guys *never* pass me notes. Study hall is soooo *boring*!" Her giggle faded from my ears as she walked into the school. Esther had hair exactly like that when she was in sixth grade. Seeing that bobbing hair, I was seeing my daughter. It came to me that half a decade had passed by, while I sat parked in that same spot, day after day. I did not have to do anything to make the time walk so quickly forward.

I just had to drive my bus, eat with my family, and the kids grew up.

Just like that.

I looked out the window on my left. A couple of Canadian geese strolled through the sparse grass adjacent to the parking lot. Yep, geese had been there every day, for ten years, twenty years—no, *thirty years*. I looked down at my jacket, the one I wore until weather turned really, really cold. It was my favorite: the brown corduroy. I had worn that heavy coat thirty years.

I smiled at each kid who stepped off my bus. I could tell their minds were transitioning, racing to the next thing. Their feet leapt off the final step, leaving bus world behind, and walking or running toward teachers' instructions and classroom friends.

As I drove home from work that day, I tried to remember everything I could about Esther in junior high. She was a good student, my Esther. That was why she was going to be an English teacher after university.

One week later, we got a call from her.

"Hello, this is Brukers."

"Hi, Dad. It's me!"

I could tell there was a smile on her face. "Hi, sweetheart! How are things going over there? Are you doing okay? Do you have some friends down there now? How is the food?"

"Um, yeah! Things are good. I'm sorry, I can't talk long. Can I talk to Mom, really quick—I have to ask her who wrote this one book. Then I really do need to get back to studying. Western Civ. It's a Gen Ed class, you know?"

"Oh, hey. What about this poor schmuck? Can't you ask me? No, kidding, fine, fine. Yeah! I'll get Mom. You take care, honey! And we'll see you in a few weeks."

Sunday evening I was lying in bed, propped up on two pillows, while Ellie tidied things throughout the room. She would often straighten my pile of books on the floor, beside the bed. They were all war books. That was all I read, besides the newspaper and *Time* magazine. I enjoyed reading about World War I, World War II, Vietnam. I read about the War of 1812 and about the Civil War. My favorites were books about undeniably compassionate wins, noble wins, of smaller forces or larger forces in far-off places, in or near tiny countries I had never before heard of.

Ellie fussed with the curtains, then crawled under the covers with her *Ladies' Home Journal*.

"Do you miss her much these days?" she said.

I looked up from my war book, that week on the Salvation Army's role in the Vietnam War. "Yeah. Sometimes. I think about her time to time. I'm just happy if she's happy. And I think she is happy there."

Ellie, frustrated with her pillows, eventually sank back beside me. "Well, I miss her lots. Every. Day."

I studied Ellie's glasses with the string attached and wrapped behind her neck. I studied her soft bangs, her thin fingers that clasped the edges of her magazine. I noticed her nail polish was wearing off. Then I nodded.

But she did not see my nod. She was trying to fix the pillow behind her neck again.

Finally, our girl came home. Ellie and I were between the yellow-painted walls of our kitchen when our daughter opened the door, suitcase in hand. Esther looked a little disoriented. There was a weird, intense pause, and nobody moved. Then Ellie rushed to the door and grabbed the suitcase, throwing her other arm around Esther.

"Welcome home, honey! How was your drive?"

Esther smiled faintly at us and half-stepped toward me. I think she wanted to hug me. I held open my arms and gave her a quick hug. "Good to see you," I said with gusto.

"Drive was fine." She stood still another moment. "I suppose Jason is watching TV downstairs?"

Ellie and I laughed nervously. "Of course," Ellie said.

Esther looked around the kitchen at all the heart decorations, like she'd never seen them before. Since the first day of our marriage, Ellie had been collecting hearts. Most of them had congregated in the kitchen. We had heart placemats, wooden heart plaques on the walls with poems engraved in them, heart-shaped hot pads, heart coasters, and heart cookie cutters sitting on top of the cupboards. Esther kept looking around at all the hearts. We watched her.

Ellie moved to the counter, began fussing with the coffee pot. "I'm sure you've eaten supper by now. But we have our lasagna. Jim 'n' I just ate. Wait—your cafeteria food must be very different. Hm. You maybe don't want this lasagna? Perhaps we could drink a little coffee together. Talk a little, or something."

I nodded, and Esther moved toward a chair. Thoughtfully, she hefted the heavy backpack off her back.

"Oh, Esther! Can you show me what books you're reading?" Ellie's face shone with a broad smile.

Esther's eyes brightened. "Sure." And she leaned into the zipper and searched through dark caves to find the right book.

She looked tired and still a little dazed. Her hair was longer, a little more scraggly, thinner looking. Her face had rounded a little, or else it was my imagination. There was something new behind her eyes. A sort of intensity, like some levers or knobs were turning back there, more than they used to. It seemed her mind was somewhere else, or partly somewhere else. The coffee pot started groaning, and Ellie joined us at the table. Another long pause, and Ellie fidgeted with the corner of a placemat.

"We got some kids, about your age, starting to drive bus now . . . but you don't want to hear about some boring old bus drivers in Alexandria. Tell us about college."

And as she began to tell us, I found myself cozier than ever before in that kitchen chair. I sank back deeper. I was not even meaning to, but I was letting go of work, as I listened: all forms of work, every form of effort. Her insights and observations began to wash over me like a shower after a hot day's shift. The entire sun sat quietly on the edge of our kitchen window beyond Esther's shoulder, and I was, well, learning. Learning, in a really passive way—and so proud of my grown-up little girl. I did not realize how tired I was feeling up till that point. But even so, all my weariness melted away in minutes.

The gears behind Esther's eyes continued to turn and search at new angles. Her mind was concentrating, working. My girl's eyes were seeing something, but what she was seeing was clearly elsewhere.

"Lo, though I walk through the valley of the shadow of death, I will fear no evil, for you are with me. Your rod and staff will comfort me." Sitting in the grass, my back against our cabin wall, near to the village of Pyramid, I gazed at the distant valley. I was a college sophomore in a semester abroad program with the Dani in West Papua (formerly Irian Jaya), Indonesia. White, streamlined clouds sat in the spaces between peaks of the blue-grey mountains, while a dense fog filled all the spaces between the distant valley and me.

That day the other fifteen students and I commenced our six-day trek. We were to leave our remote jungle village, Pyramid, and journey into even more remote villages. Our destination: Silimo. This semester abroad program wasn't the run-of-the-mill classroom experience. Rather, it was designed as a risky adventure program and apprenticeship.

The six-day trek, in my mind, unfortunately afforded plenty of opportunity for something to go wrong, for someone to get injured with no hospital in sight. When I had embarked on day one of the program—that August of '97—climbing onto the first aircraft of our many flight connections toward Irian Jaya, I knew it was very possible I could die before Christmas.

Thoughts and fears of dying (poisonous snake bite, being kidnapped by extremists, our small aircraft crashing on her route back to Pyramid, to name a few concerns) were hovering near me as I glimpsed again the fog in the distance. We said our good-byes at the missionary compound: to the students who were too ill to join us, and to the Dani and American program staff who kept watch over them. And then we simply started walking.

We walked and we walked, through the hidden soul of West Papua's ominous passes and her trickiest valleys, passing village after village. Villages embedded in the steep mountainsides, like little pebbles embedded in a soft gravel road. Villages where time stood still, pooled, seemed to settle.

As we walked, we heard low-voiced chants resounding from various grass huts and nearby fire pits, songs that fit their environment like the sound of campers' voices and banter fit the Boundary Waters Canoe Area of Minnesota. Air stood pure, still, unpolluted. Each meadow region spanned a wide expanse, and each new hilltop horizon let us glimpse another chain of rising and falling mountains.

This six-day trek embodied the journey of life all wrapped up within our teenage hiking boots and those tiny huts. The experience marched before my mind's eye as a series of colorful metaphors for any "journey" attempted in one's life—complete with the obstacles, blessings, pains, and pleasures. Long, rickety wooden suspension bridges, connecting one mountain ridge to another, hung perilously over white, roaring rapids, upholding us in the same way a thin wisp of faith would save us from wages of sin.

One day we came across two bridges that paralleled each other. Both were hovering five hundred meters above the caps of the raging, white waters below. One of the bridges proved to be sturdy, straight, and strong—the planks all lined up neatly, one after the other. Bridge two was leaning sideways, and planks stood out at severe angles. A large number of planks were, in fact, missing. We all felt much relief and gratitude to opt for walking across the sturdy bridge!

We walked farther. We crossed streams and shallow rivers; then, after another three hours of hiking, we'd cross many more streams, more rivers. Sometimes, a few of our Dani friends insisted on carrying me and others across the faster currents or through the higher rapids. Students' legs grew tired. Our skin stank, our hair was fast gaining grease, the edges of our pant legs held more mud and puddle water, and toilets didn't exist as part of the picture. More muscles ached, and the miles stretched on and on.

Why do people love "the journey"? I think it's because we really like learning something ourselves, rather than listening to someone explain the world to us. I also think we enjoy testing our strength, determining whether or not we are capable of rising to a challenge. Primarily, I think we love the relief that comes at the end of any journey. I think we love the cool drink or sweet breeze which only feels more welcome because we surmounted, endured, something rigorous or harsh.

Day five of our journey through the southeastern highlands of West Papua was the toughest. We began hiking a little after dawn, and our plan included reaching the location where yet another tribe would meet us, and where we'd tent overnight. We ascended and descended with the mountain peaks and valleys, watching the earth come to life in the colors of West Papua: lime-green mountains, brown and gold mud puddles, and the rainbow colors of flowers clinging to trees. Grass and trees were wet with dew and for many hours the wet foliage scratched our bare brown or white legs, as we wove our way along the Sekerli Mountains' rough trails.

Fat, lengthy tree roots were each exposed to the moist air and then mangled and tangled with one another. Bubbling streams meandered around and between the trees, deep in the island's heart. The branches and leaves formed a dark canopy over our heads. Landscapes, that fifth day, resembled scenery from Tolkein's *The Lord of the Rings*. Was a sight including bright green slopes, giant, towering clusters of deep chocolate-brown trees, and murky shadows sinking mysteriously between heavy and full, fruit-laden stems; it spoke to me, "The Kingdom of Heaven is here. Not just to come . . ."

Rain began at noon.

This earth contains a little bit of hell also, I was reminded on that fifth day. Just before our troupe neared the final leg of our route, massive flooding had apparently washed over it, making our intended section impassable. It was necessary to take a detour, which was much, much longer. The trail became more muddy and slippery, and then we reached the foot of the never-ending mountain.

We climbed the base of "never-ending mountain" through Tolkein's trees, in the rain, using rocks and roots as stepping stones, relishing the beauty but starting to wonder why we hadn't reached the top yet. Up and up, up and up, up and up.

Up and up, up and up, up and up.

Finally we reached the summit.

We then went down the far side. Down and down, down and down.

Down and down, down and down. In the mud, each inch of the way, we were stepping, striding, slopping, and slipping. "So is it close—or still a few more hours?" one student asked our trek leader.

"We're almost there!" he shouted from the front of the line. "About an hour!"

"Are we getting close?" another teen hollered—after what seemed like many more hours had passed.

"We're almost there! About an hour!" Our Papuan friends and guides were supplying their best estimates to our trek leader, though, naturally, the Papuan perspectives on time are extremely different from Americans' views of time. The forest and jungle grew darker, the trail grew muddier, our legs found more foliage to scratch against. When well over an hour passed and we still hadn't reached the next Ngalik hosts at the tenting site, disappointment began to sit heavily on me like a second soaking backpack. It felt as though someone told me I must return to the start, make an entire day's journey again. My grip on the hiking stick produced painful blisters. Blind under the darkness, and unsure of our footing on "never-ending mountain," we sank into deep mud, trying to step from rock to rock.

It was definitely night. "Is it quite awhile still, or are we getting close?" I tried.

"We're almost there! About an hour!" our trek guide called in reply.

Frustration, like the disappointment, added a harsher heaviness, wearing thin my emotions and my resolve. To hear that my relief would surely be one hour away, and then to find this not to be true, messed with my thoughts, changed things in my mind. I ran out of pep talks or positive thoughts. To not know where the end of the trail was (or if there was any end at all), was a big perseverance problem. One that inherently made it hard for all of us to "pace ourselves."

Back at home, I could run the 800-meter dash *all out* because I knew that the pain and strain was gone in less than two and a half minutes. Back at home, I could handle getting dirty with barn chores and mucking out stalls, because I knew I could jump in the shower soon as I wanted or needed to. But on this mountain there was no relief, no hope realized, no end— it seemed. I saw on that night how important hope is for our survival, and how often I'd previously been hinging on it in my daily life.

So I had a choice to make, inside the mud and swelling darkness. I could either continue to hold my breath, as it were, for the relief, for the end—or I could figure out a way to manipulate my psyche to enjoy the actual pain, present dirt, and current rain. Joy in the pain.

Finally, we saw a tiny train of torches decorating the darkness far below. Children and adults, decked in what appeared to be banana-leaf raincoats, made their way toward this wet hiking ensemble, to guide us out of the trees and off the slopes. Our newest escorts, Ngalik residents of the Amikma Valley, indeed were clad in pandanus-leaf rain capes (the capes positioned on the heads to protect their bodies from rain, and to leave arms and hands free for scrambling up steep trails). The moment they reached us, they took our mixed group (Sentani residents, American folk, and Pyramid residents) swiftly by the hand. Literally, our hands were held by our smiling, ecstatic guides. Carefully and lovingly, our companions then led each one of us down the hazardous trail to the elusive mountain end. So there really *was* an end, a floor! Relief.

We had been hiking the Sekerli Mountains for sixteen hours straight.

We were led to a fire that was a heartwarming celebration of hospitality, community, and also simply the comfort of heat! There, before midnight on day five, we touched the end soil and completed our great trek across the southeastern highlands of West Papua.

People so often refer to life as "a journey," as mentioned earlier. Huh. At least twice in one essay. Perhaps this tendency of ours flows from our love of the unknowns around each next bend. Even for people who don't really revel in risks or surprises, it's quite possible that these are events which the subconscious mind and soul of *every* living being wants, or needs.

The next morning, only a short walk remained. As we crossed the bridge marking the entrance to Silimo village, even more children eagerly greeted our muddy crew of travelers. In the steady rain—wearing nothing but their pandanus-leaf raincoats, a couple of girls with grass skirts, and a few of the boys in gourds—Ngalik friends danced, swaying from side to side in an enthusiastic welcoming celebration. Arms flapping, hips swinging, voices pitching and sinking, the children sang from deep in their chest, filling the air with a sound I cannot put down on paper. I really cannot describe it—the sight nor the sound. But I can still remember how they powerfully and beautifully harmonized, how our welcome committee chanted and danced, how they *sang*.

And I can repeat it, echo it.

The memories now lie like a profound secret in my heart, and are still maturing me, as I learn of hope, and learn of *song*.

Road Trip: A Minnesotan Travels through Montana

five people there she laughs as I say I've arrived in Montana
I'm greeted only by Shania Twain and a bluegrass singer

they go with us melancholy and sunny
with the winking grin of the wild sunflowers and the low sleeping mountains
blue lazy dewdrops on the rim of Montana's thirsty floor

eighteen hours of yellow lines and peeling tar
we know a land with ten thousand lakes
and our maps again take us home

but the awesome emptiness of the big sky and yellow thirsty floor pull me into their
yawning contentedness and it's suddenly once again easy to believe the journey is the destination

behind us the whir of Washington's hikers and hippies
Starbucks and sailboats
transients and traffic
before us the daily life and daily bread

what is the point

maybe these mountains in Montana and the cozy way they match the men in the Exxon station
and the way these men with their cowboy hats and cigarettes match the twangy music
which soaks every thistled station on our radio today

eyes wide open I yawn with that yonder blue valley and that low yellow hill
I swallow the bluegrass twang and sleepy sunflowers
                                        to find Minnesota still in me
                                                . . . and still fiercely driving

Women

A fresh smile lights up the shadow
cast by the scarves and skyscrapers of Kabul,

and the story of Christina Rossetti's
brush with the male intellectuals

of her frilly and hypocritical era
reaches the pages of a textbook

read by a young woman who knows
she's got it pretty good. Things change,

and yet that same young woman
teaches tennis lessons to a group

of kids, girls sitting down on the
hot, spongy surface, because they

don't want the boys in class to
see them miss still another easy shot.

The First Lady, tall and careful
in her long, turquoise ballroom dress,

uses her speck in the spotlight
to sit in a library and read children's books.

But few adults are watching her
or listening to her plea for social justice

as their eyes and ears are tuned
only to the flashing tan stomachs,

juvenile smiles, and often-empty lyrics
of media's pop stars and the nation's porn.

a silent incubation that erupts with screaming
unwelcome vomit forms a lonely perseverance
and the tearing brings more labor unseen

women who are mothers find hope in enjoying
the infants and the spit-up and the knee-biters' kisses
a silent incubation that erupts with screaming

parents in conflict—then again a midnight feeding
so she must cry upward for a heavenly response
and the tearing brings more labor unseen

unknowns give flight to a fast-pulsed roaring
birth proves worse than terror's first glance
a silent incubation that erupts with screaming

no witness gives nod to the pain in her resting
seems a miracle to stand while feeling so nauseous
and the tearing brings more labor unseen

paycheck has stopped—yet to-do lists are growing
she's lovingly stripped of sweet self-dependence
a silent incubation that erupts with screaming
and the tearing brings more labor unseen

1. Husband
2. Growth
3. Pain
4. Warmth
5. Stretching
6. Internal
7. Stretching
8. Bradley classes
9. Different exercises
10. New friends
11. Pain
12. Pain
13. Joy
14. Sleeping positions
15. Love
16. Discouragement
17. Labor PAIN
18. Neck injuries
19. More laundry
20. More laundry
21. Husband's family of origin
22. Neck injuries
23. Mommy wars
24. Love
25. Loving
26. Sloppy clothing
27. Neck pain
28. Schedules
29. Smile
30. Giving help and asking for help
31. Misunderstood and misunderstandings
32. Time
33. Bedrooms
34. Mommy breaks
35. My family of origin

36. Neck pain

37. Schedules

38. Pumping

39. Exhaustion

40. Exhaustion

41. More dishes

42. Self-care

43. Love

44. Strong sense of not measuring up . . . in so many different ways

45. Criticism

46. More cooking

47. A lot of walks

48. Gratefulness

49. Marriage

50. Another child?

Stretching in a Strange Glow

Soft morning light came through cabin blinds
as my cousin and I inhaled thirty small Swedish pancakes.
Measurable feats in those preteen years were
part of the fun and the light
of being alive.
Laughter rose from our blonde heads
and the steaming stacks
while stomachs were stretching

only a bit.

Then, a couple of decades later
something stretched beyond belief.
Our hearts became

more hearts … more mouths … and eight hands.
Grabbing, hungry, kicking, emerging, delivering … avidly licking syrup.

What utterly immeasurable milestones
were those blond boys
inside of my cousin and me.

Eating, drowning, delighting
in so many more of life's gifts
        than those thirty simple pancakes
            … than just the old games … from mothers' youth.

Tired Expressions

The exhaustion
during those first six weeks was

> too sore and rich,
> too ripe and absurd,
> too stark real,
> too abundantly fruitful,
> too faithfully serving,
> too rare and adoring,
> too aware of brilliance,
> too basely important,
> too infinitely and imminently crucial

to complain about.
For that tiredness, for that time, words may fail me.

> I cannot give a true account.

On the Bit

and this is where we are all going
from chasing wind to most respectful bowing

harnessed power
our relationship with God
on the bit
our goal

rider and horse now one

perfect submission   no one was conquered
no one is straining
energy pushing toward forward
toward
no behavior change   no outward adjustments
nor adornments
solely an inner yielding

western   eastern   muscles   supple
we are horse
God is communicating

we are comfortable and compliant   needing only light commands
responding to the lightest touch

impulsion back to front

          and at one gentle cue, willing to run with our Rider directly
                    into the battle

Wheat Dies

Dust dances
behind the window's light

but a heart breaks every day.

We can only see it if we stare at the dust dancing.

You and I
feel a tear well up
remembering old dust,
kicked awake.

Aching feelings,
noble and beautiful,

but almost always overlooked.
Partially hidden.   As with losing our lives
to find life:
a maxim as nostalgic and ancient as one old, worn Bible.
Yes, rest

at times.

Fragrant promises of old dust
later this evening will move sparkling stars.
The extra-full hours,

the overloaded schedules,
stretching and serving
can produce promise
as surely as the harvest

later

of this one small grain of wheat,
already sleeping,
dying deeply in the ground,

is saving our lives.

But the Bugs

Our first infant is now resting with his father
and I am with the Mississippi and with everything
rising above her steam.

Sunset steals a peek atop brown water and brown banks
and I,
one tired mom out of millions,
I am free to steal a stroll, steal a pause,
alone.

      The thoughts are beautiful and bristly as they fly at me,

light-hearted and heavily burdened.

    The gnats jab at my

eyelids   —so swift

        on my ear—

    so annoying!

I rest on a bench and stare at the river banks

   —but the bugs.   But the tiny things sparkling!
—like scattered dew—

     —between the sunset and my line of sight—

           between stress and twilight serenity.
      In their sophomoric glory,
   in their speed, the motion produces beauty.

       Though they go nowhere, they are creating energy as they spend it.
In watching them stir, my teeming heart is soothed with silent awe . . .

       —The tiny things sparkling.

A Cooking Hausfrau:

   in Tragicomic Celebration of Otherness and I, Worth and They

"Good" cooking . . . her way, his way
                    . . . my way?
Joy and strength, last drops of energy, blended in . . .
and tears

falling
        out.

Occasionally his way, somebody's way

. . . my way?

Exhausted humans,
misunderstandings.
Visitors . . . and who has value? And what did you say was valuable? What do I say?

Yet,
all young brides have stunning and awe-inspiring abilities to pour our spent hearts
into sometimes hidden work, into unending house chores.

Where do tears go if not into a soup? How to smile if sharp angles are at home?

Now
I pour out the sweet perfume of more meals
and the mother-love of my mixing
into our oven.

To let things roll off, to shake off what sounds a lot like another's disdain, I laugh
        —faster. I focus more on my work "outside" of the home and then—
                back within our own kitchen.   —Make again fragrant, baked heat floating
                        more frequently—
out of
our oven
and into
him, her, others . . .

into Me.

Round
Spring on Earth

And the green of the buds

pulses brighter than ever before

Once again

And you forget that you remember

who your sister is

Once again

And the only choice you can make

is to make family a priority

Once again

And the Master Lover blows kisses t'ward you

—friends crossing near your path—

Once again

And the transcendent laughs

as you attempt to put it down on paper

—you being a gleeful, half-blind human

And Israeli Jews' borders tragically conflict

with the borders of Palestinian Arabs

Heartbreakingly again

And that dollar you kept

is withheld from you

Once again

And the green of the buds

pulses brighter than ever before

Once again

What Is a Smile?

I have tried and I have quit.
I have confessed the hurt as well as denied the hurt.
I have turned away and I have pursued.
I have smiled from my heart,
and I have smiled with my will.

Yet each of these pathways weave
only
dissonance in an already distorted design,
and the pattern fails.

Someday when he steps confidently over the crowded half-truths, the long miles
of our many messy rooms,
with his best smile, utter honesty,
willing, meaning
only for me; unplanned acceptance engaged

. . . then, I, with my heart, can.

Real smile of a happy heart,
genuinely turned, spontaneously planned.

What Is Truth?
at Very Least, a Sphere

A roommate of mine in college once said to me: "I feel like I'm just scratching the surface of God and the Bible. Like on the brink of getting to know Him—but then realizing I'm only scratching the surface." I've never forgotten those impromptu words. And for whatever reason, each time I think about them, I picture a ball in her hands.

Truth as a sphere.

My literature classmates, college professors, and I often discussed the difference between "Big T Truth" and "little t truth." We considered the Big T Truth to be God the Creator, including the invisible Spirit and the visible man, Jesus. We analyzed myriads of little t truths embedded in novels, our lives, and shorts stories. We encountered truths about the human experience, philosophical truths, and truths about family. In science classes especially, I encountered many little t truths; gravity is unmistakably true and math equations are unshakably factual.

In each of these encounters with Truth and truth, it often seems we're merely scratching the surface. Seeing only the outer, outer core of something . . . something spherical.

I can't seem to shake this mind picture of a globe.

We who are made in God's image are large enough to hold a little globe in our hands, as we would hold a book, a baby, or a map. And so many colors, cultures, truths, and possibilities are held in that little globe. Simultaneously, God is standing who-knows-where and He's "got the whole world in His hands." Earth is just one of the small globes He cups inside His fingertips.

While we scratch the surface of getting to know our Father in Heaven, He unpeels us. He discovers new ways to show us that we are the apple of His eye. And when we let Him, He gently strips away layers of our baggage, our sin, and our self-protective measures, to tenderly point out our blind spots. More importantly, He wants to let us see what He sees: our strengths, talents, and gifts. We are still unpacking the riddle of Him, while He continues to decipher the mystery of us.

My husband and I hope to nurture faith and love for God in our kids. We hope to set our kids on Jesus' path. That's one of our big dreams right now. We try to communicate our own encounters with God, confess our own failures, and teach through example. But with each question a child throws at me—about God, or His Son, or God's relationship with earthlings—it's like my faith takes two steps backwards. I sometimes can come up with answers. Sometimes not. I feel I'm only scratching the surface.

I read *A Wrinkle in Time* a few times in my childhood, and as an adult I've appreciated the film rendition. *A Wrinkle in Time* helps me again to be aware of the unending number of neighboring galaxies. The Milky Way that our globe floats in is not the only galaxy in outer space. Millions more galaxies, stacked upward, sideways, and inside out, onward toward infinity. Somewhere within those spaces, God and Heaven are established, along with myriads of angels, singing to Jesus. And here on earth, in the broken, humble hearts, in the glass of water shared in Jesus' name, within our souls when we invite Jesus to come near and be in charge of us, in the cold or hungry bodies and souls of homeless people—God dwells on earth, too. And the Holy Spirit—the ghost-like manifestation of God—as unconfined and mysterious as the wind in our own troposphere. God's place-of-residence list is a massively long list, yet it is still somehow difficult to explain to my son, daughter, or to myself *where* exactly God *is*.

Or *who* He is. There's another riddle. He is "I Am" (Exodus 3:14). He's another person at the meeting, whenever two people gather in His Name (Matthew 18:20). He is visible to us in His ocean-art. He is we and we are Him, when we bring hope or liberation to the marginalized or oppressed. He is fire in the burning bush (Exodus 3:2). He is a consuming fire that will incinerate whatever does not bear good fruit—branch or human (Deuteronomy 4:24, Matthew 3:10). He is a friend (John 15:15). The Lord *is*, yet our minds cannot fully understand how or who.

Some of us who believe the Bible, and try to live out its message, will continue to discover, will spend the rest of our earthly lives trying to uncover, what's in there. Inside its pages, there resides infinitely more to study. Room to grow in how we interpret, understand, and unravel the texts, and unending numbers of newer insights, which we can attempt to apply and obey in daily life.

Still scratching the surface. None of us will ever master a complete understanding of each nation or culture, nor will any of us learn every single way that exists on planet earth—of cooking, praying, decorating, "doing life." (There is no best way.)

And in the journeys of marriage and motherhood, there are so many practical truths— such as how to live in a more peaceful dynamic with one's spouse. Relational skills: such as how to listen *even* better, for example, or learning which techniques are effective in helping young siblings to get along.

Relaxation practices, mothering routines, strategies to live a balanced life, relational skills—

these are little t truths I cannot live without. Good to hang on to these. Nice also to keep an open mind and learn from the people around me. There are hundreds of various ways to plan a holiday, grill a steak, select a school, or walk from one end of the forest to another. And it's always refreshing to remind ourselves when dealing with difficult people: Just because someone is always strong-willed does not necessarily mean that he or she is always right. The truth will stand (and humbly).

One of my favorite scenes in the New Testament—and perhaps one of the most paradoxical—is of Jesus standing face to face with Pilate. Pilate whose political clout could have Jesus either hanged or absolved. Jesus whose flames of power are warming the core of the earth and flickering below Pilate's feet. Consuming fire.

"Pilate said to Him, 'So . . . you are a king, then?'" (John 18:37 NASB, KJB, NIV).

Jesus answered, "You say correctly that I am a king. For this I have been born, and for this I have come into the world, to testify to the truth. Everyone who is of the truth hears My voice" (John 18:37 NASB 1995).

Pilate said to Him, "What is truth?" (John 18:38).

John 14:6 quotes Jesus announcing, "I am . . . the Truth."

Pilate looks directly at the man who had once declared himself to be all truth personified, and asks him point-blank: "What is truth?" I adore this scene! This conversation here, involving the politician and the carpenter, is in itself a mystery that will take us millions of years to fully comprehend.

In the book of Revelations, Jesus is our beloved husband. Our kind King and successful military leader. A breathing Morning Star among stars.

. . . Stars we barely see as we plant our feet on the earth, circular stars flying at us with their old age, their backwards years, and their presence.

. . . Spherical stars that spread out eternally, third cousins of other stars, within their own cousin-galaxies.

Other galaxies of which we are barely scratching the surface.

Yet

all curving toward us

or away,

and all so true.

World Hunger

Wholeness is pursuing my thoughts and toes.
Then why am I hustling, hurrying, grabbing . . .
                    simply to give you milk, give you help?

My mother's milk
began my broken pursuit of our usual and unusual hungers.

Freezer Full of Milk

With my first baby, I ran into some major kinks to be worked out in the breastfeeding schedule. While I was figuring out doses and pumping routines, I produced so much extra milk that our freezer became overloaded, crammed full of my own milk. Somehow, between my newness, eagerness, and my avid supply, I constantly created more milk. I then realized I could feed starving children in far-off places, with milk from my own body as the one and only resource. This, as one could imagine, was a strange discovery. I'm still unfolding and unpacking the thought.

Sure, I anticipated many challenges inherent in this new role as Mommy. I knew there'd be a few sleepless nights. I knew that I'd be nursing babies during the night.

Six head injuries in three years. Quite hard bangs. Why? Mothers know that we focus enormously on the kids . . . but was I so self-neglecting that my primary doctor had to tell me (twice) that I should wear a helmet full-time? Three of those six head injuries were "laundry-related." Really? I saw a neuorologist and he ordered an MRI of my brain. The brain is unbruised—great news—but the neurologist encouraged me to research sleep hygiene, chia, and nutrition. Laundry catastrophes only exemplify what can happen to women if we let self-care slide, even for a moment, choosing to care about the kids before caring about ourselves.

Motherhood. Tougher than any marathon.

I didn't know how tricky it would become to take half-decent care of myself during this time. Prior to motherhood, I had always enjoyed outdoor adventures, and I was quite content with low-key meals, sweaty clothes, athletic challenges, and minimal grooming.

Becoming a mother has made me so high-maintenance. Or maybe: made me aware of how high-maintenance a woman ought to be. I think it is ridiculous that some days I've had to convince myself that I deserve five minutes: to put on deodorant, do something stylish with my hair, or complete a few neck stretches or physical therapy. Even to secure just thirty minutes for writing a poem or an essay involved multiple days of searching for the right opportunity when my kids could be otherwise safely distracted, aka child care.

Who knew I'd need to incorporate spinach—urgently—into my diet? I flourished in basketball, barn work, tennis, and track, before becoming pregnant, without eating a single gram of spinach. Enter motherhood: our babies drank so much of my iron that I frequently needed to eat beef, spinach, chicken—just to keep my iron levels from becoming dangerously low.

Before motherhood, I generally delighted in being on time for things—early, actually. I tried to be clean and responsible—often washing all the dishes before going to bed. Maybe check emails or Facebook after that? Not anymore. Not if I wanted to groom my sleep hygiene. Doctors advised me to go to bed earlier, since the kids would wake us much earlier. Sleep deprivation confronted my husband and me each time our babies and toddlers became sick. Illness-induced bronchospasm and childhood asthma were in our offspring; sadly, our kids ran into breathing trouble too many times.

Sleep hygiene and good nutrition became for me a soothing balm. I wanted to research them more. I wanted to embrace them more. I got my husband involved. We've both been experimenting with creative napping options.

My body refuses to sleep at night if I don't make time for a rigorous workout within that day. My body feels so empty, so abandoned, and so incapable if I don't eat eggs, green vegetables, or meat in a day.

Interesting to think about: in our workaholic society, could it be that women and nursing mothers aren't the only people needing this kind of well-thought-out sleep? And could it be that more green or red vegetables would also aid young men and old men to think more clearly, feel more joy, have more hope?

Many women come to this or similar realizations upon entering motherhood, that there's a change in our definition of self-sacrifice. From a discipline of monastic scarcity, toward a lifestyle full of warmth and blankets. From moderation and self-restraint, toward a new focus on fruitful abundance, thick milk. Caring for the hungry not by eating less, but by eating more. Rather than investing in cold courage: now aiming to be more soft, vulnerable, snuggly. An entirely different approach to our historical or initial understanding of sacrificial love.

We care for our family best by caring for ourselves—*not* any longer through denying ourselves. Yes, even taking romantic dates out with the husband. Not because we're selfish or spoiled. Yes, being taken "out" on dates, because if the marriage isn't healthy, then the health of an entire family unit wanes in grave ways.

Days when I was home with my sick toddlers, I noticed the battle. I could see I was caught between thriving and crashing; fighting the cloud of sleep deprivation, whenever another icky hour rose up to challenge me.

The minute-by-minute dependence on God is a dance of survival, a labor of love, which many busy mothers have come to know well. But *before* the woman goes crazy, she needs some time to herself. She needs a hearty breakfast, earlier marriage moments, earlier bedtimes, and Vitamin D in whatever way, shape, or form. How silly of us rugged, resourceful, or athletic women, who used to believe we could do just fine without comforts.

Six mild head traumas in three years. Ouch. But the good news: with my own milk, I will feed the world. Spending more extensive time in the kitchen to prepare a well-rounded, healthy lunch is the new fasting. Pampering myself with sleep hygiene, yoga, and leafy greens is the new marathon. Lying down for at least thirty minutes a day is the new happy pill. And I won't feel guilty for being so high-maintenance, or for napping. These came along with the job, apparently—written into my assignment, long before the complicated lady I am today

was even born.

Splintering Thoughts

approaching a serene bend in the fog

  gratefully
   on a cross-country ski trail

    if there is a quiet second in this day
      between tick
        toddler
         tock
          infant
           tick
            husband
             tock
perhaps just one thought could complete

      separation of my hopes and my statements
        —split neurons of my questions
                splitting like ice chopped—
      ice chopped
—pieces of my mind—
   firing fiercely outward directionless

                meeting the invasions every minute
              head-on and surprised
                like snowflakes and hail and bitter wind finding and slapping my face
              sending my original thoughts spinning
                  lost

my son

                    toddling
              my husband   busy
        and a newborn daughter needing constant care

                      growing, stretching, expanding
        ice shrinking my original path
         tar forever changed
          street not the same
           as it is
          chopped again, flattened by one

       ski run
     fiercely hoping that I am
approaching a serene bend in the fog

Calling Mommy

inside and outside
my calling is calling
i hear him and know him
crawling soprano up our stairs
as he calls my name and looks for me
our heart finds itself
our home rises tall

what was lost is found

i've now been appropriately named
labeled and titled
placed in a fun but frumpier box
our little knee-biter says Mommy now
pure   three-dimensional sound   wrapping
around a sweet spot
the word naively singing a miniature siren sword

piercing my ears my eyes and my heart treble clef small pitch ringing clear
with
delicate, infinite images
walking across my mind

i've been placed in a fun but frumpier box
our little knee-biter says Mommy now

as he calls my name and looks for me
our heart finds itself
our home rises tall

what was lost is found

Mommy

Lukas' Photo, Age 1½:
        an American Cinquain

Somehow
Lukas holds old and
young together with his
sigh on rainy days. Eyes laughing
and blue.

Timber Caught

Part I:

Hours pass by us,
like heavying timber.
To adore my own child—what wonder!
My living baby . . . needs *me*

yet through logs I can barely see
a sleep spinning
and wondering
. . . where is slumber?
Current so fast, if I look back . . .
while in the present a confusing

slow   pack.

This stream . . . bringing pieces of trees   drifting   by,
the feeding, logs jamming, timber crowding. Cry,

heavying timber. A longing

. . . for slumber.
Days drifting by as gifts,

yet   without refreshment.

Skills halting and new. Routine shaken
while one old rhythm is dying.
Slivers of logs, spinning, a rapid and fresh wave of life crying   vying
for a cluttered me.
Screaming and singing new thoughts
new calendars, she and I.

For later flowing. A new free.

Part II:
Two Tankas

The branches flow slow.
I clean I nurture. I try
to be joyful. Tired.
Branches that form jams and piles.
Timber swirling, and backwards.

With a push—to mature.
Timber *cracks*. Then drifts along by
in a river where self dies.
This stretching, this pushing, this current
catches debris, spins me, swirls me, again free.

"When we pray to God we must be seeking nothing

—nothing."

—ST. FRANCIS OF ASSISI—

There, by the River

he and I
wanted an outdoor wedding

                 there

along the banks of the Ottertail River
a living river witnessed our marriage

there was rain, a river, and a sliver of sun

days and winters faded   new days arrived
         we had babies   and children

two children joined the excitement, expecting our new creation

inside of me, at nine weeks, he or she died   we gave a name

and placed Vita Bergren in a small white box

husband, wife, son, daughter together created a memorial service

then

    we bade all sad, deep goodbyes   watched our third
       as the bright appearances of him or her
         disappeared confidently and expectantly
          down the Mississippi River

       surrounded in our sun's sparkles
         and with one day's brilliant beam swirling over the surface
          of many brown, dark waters

he and I began with an outdoor wedding
near a slow country river

but we could not have known that later

the happy, hopeful songs
and our unborn baby

would all eventually

float away

there

Sailboat

Coming about.
So hormones rise, fade, quell, and shoot. Mother Nature does things. Things like shining.
        Things like breaking branches. Things like severe *increase* in windspeed.

She
        said that she will influence maneuverability,
but does she choose things?   Wind.
                                    Was it intentional? Every time.

Yes, there exists the gorgeous, gorgeous meaning of white-capped waves and blue-black waves,
        and the comprehension of the missed turn.

Mainsail and jib appearing as round as and embowed as waves when snared in stormy weather.
        When full of life and breath—

                        when wind coming from north
or left.

Tears and sad feelings did not come daily nor did they come in any pattern at all.

More
like the squall.

        Sudden, surprising, unwelcome storm. A captain and his ship
            cannot plan a sudden squall at sea. The squall changes compass and we.

Changes things,
how we think. Think about us.

That boat was I (a medium-small craft: of wood, plastic, metal, nails).

One woman staring at the sky.

I had a beautiful black-and-white picture on our bedroom wall, in a
soft
blonde
wood
frame.

I often felt great pleasure to look at it. A sailboat in a squall at sea. Most miscarriages are not the
mother's fault. Not Mommy's failure,
        but the tears and the waves came as blood continued to splash over the sides
                without border.

Without border. Quelling and being quelled. Coming about. Change route.

As waves, with no sand in sight.

A sailboat for transport and also for recreation:
How do hormones explain "things"
        to one's heart?
Nothing lies flat
in a sudden squall at sea.
And in that picture framed on our red-painted bedroom wall,
        barely visible, was the captain;
                a tiny figure—a shadow trying to steer,
                        trying to manage,

                                trying to stand steady.

Father of my children, noting the weight of passengers,
        maneuvering a ship along
no
visible
path.

But,   . . . it still comes.   The heart stops beating and

we
        "come about." Change of route,
                cannot predict the sudden storm at sea
                        or the "spontaneous miscarriage" inside of me.

        How does one explain this to toddler brains, to the living
                older siblings who are anticipating new hands, new eyes? Tilting port,
then shoving rude   and starboard.

Blood splashed upon deck, upon
the brave—but insufficient—wood structure,

of a cheerfully noble frame.

Of a sailboat
strong on land
        and strong on currents.

                The sailboat looking now so delicate in the increasing force of a squeezing wind,

with the sky, left or right.
Starboard Port.
And up down.

Carrying:
a Haiku

wanting holding yes

blood and water, promises.

small body released

Shooting Star:
    a Haibun

When a particle of comet dust entered our atmosphere
    friction caused fire
        and a streak of light was born.
          When a fetus failed to thrive
            he or she became my own blood flow,
              my own flesh falling away too quickly,

                      dead life.

                This was called a shooting star.

        comets move in space

      lost dust as lost blood from womb

        to another place

Three Tanka Poems

Black Hole

If the core of an
exploded star becomes heav-
ier than three suns, it
becomes a black hole. Stars can
explode. Babies can be blood.

To My Child

Though our universe
always expands, you set in-
to motion a fast
retreat with your backwards blood,
simply by stopping your heart.

Pieces of Me
Somewhere

You are somewhere else
yet hormones still shake my frame.
My frame remembers
you. I once saw a shooting
star enter a black hole. Womb.

Ottertail and Mississippi:

Haiku

rivers dear to me

one body floating away

never to return

All Heart: Two Haikus

The first ultrasound.
When I asked what I was seeing?
White energy—Heart!

Such a fast heartbeat.
The small person was all heart.
Before it died. Heart.

Christmas Due Date

Iambic Feet

We saw the positive pregnancy test!

Ultrasound bared a glad heartbeat.

Due date would have been Christmas Day.

Then, then, then, I bled;

blood of the dying, but me, I lost.

Ultrasound a second time. We saw our tiny . . . heart-heap,

lying flat on the floor of a home within me.

Free Verse

born to die
that's what they say about Jesus Christ

my Vita Bergren died in May

wrapped dead
inside one inch of

my living flesh
my blood

born dead

born loved

born with no discoverable gender

at nine weeks old

Then the anticipated Christmas Day came
. . . and went.

Yet, Runa

Do you remember when you saw one sunbeam jump through shade to splash the wall
near you?

a wish is here
a wish went
a wish died

thankfulness is attained here

thankfulness under the bridge

Runa was three years old when our baby died
and under the soil
Yet, Runa
and floating with the debris
Yet, Runa

and I want to be even more thankful

peacefully we can accept mercy
from another hurting person
or give it

yet

. . . I have a real live daughter
as beautiful as an elf queen
smiles   laughter   sunshine
thankfulness is attained here

exercise and sunlight make many of my hours better
but my daughter enjoys nearly every hour of her life
being happy
being in pink
loving
loving purple
loving flying unicorns
and horses

sometimes I want a new baby

Yet, Runa

thankfulness across the bridge
thankfulness is attained here
thankfulness under the soil
motherhood is now
Yet, Runa

sometimes I want less neck pain
always I have pain in my neck and back, along entire left side

I want   I want
Yet . . .

the sun is skipping toward me no matter how many things are going wrong in the world
smiling   laughing
everyone can testify to a different ache

Yet, Runa's smile is so beautifully joy-filled
I must squint my eyes

Yet . . . Runa

Sunlight still reaches
everyone.

My Mom

Across table top or
across the front porch
my mom's huge, loving smile and
the deep, vibrant twinkle
in her eyes. A white

star leaping

each time

out of the blue

with a tiny, out-going
movement. Truly moving. A shooting star,
a liquid, lucid flash between her lids. Then the gleam is over and
life as usual as she reminds me
so gently

to close the doors; that it's really time to stop leaving them open.

As with her hugs, such oceans

—seas and tides
intensity and infinity
fondness
and devotion—

reside in her eyes,

even when she must remind me again.

I Remember May Day

I

        remember sensing excitement
        and hope near our front yard.

Our doorbell rings. It is spring and only a few trees seem ready.
On May Day, more buds additionally appear,
but only on the trees that already

do

hold flowers. Boys in colorful T-shirts and summer shorts
fade into the forests of our family's front yard, bringing candy
for my three sisters and me.

We all could decline even proms, could turn away these dances.
Children are running and hiding; all are smiling.
And another neighbor's home,
the sweet May memories of being pursued. Then—shadows,
and sharing life, sharing this moment, sharing May Day, and sharing our home,
with my three sisters.

I

am caught.
A kiss offered . . . turned away. Doorbell again—almost
someone.
A sense of running away.
More buds appear—but only on the branches that already

do

        hold flowers.

A Day in the Life . . .

After my own two children would not nap one sub-zero afternoon, I needed to get out to see the sunset—soak up the brisk, blue sky after some Minnesota blizzards. Walter, my husband, was presently at his last day of class for the semester, studying public health at the University of Minnesota.

After intense shoveling and scraping, my toddlers and I were able to load up and launch out of our wintery driveway. Soon we could see past the city skyscrapers to gaze at the orange sky—beauty coaxing us west. We had a nice, brief, gorgeous hike along the Mississippi parkway, just the three of us, extremely bundled in our snow clothes, relishing the softness of the two feet of snow we inherited in the past forty-eight hours! Unfortunately, our adventure and our trail were nowhere near any porta-potties.

I finally managed to get both screaming kids back into the car. They had either hurt themselves or wound up with wet snow on vulnerable patches of skin. By this point I had to go No. 1, and badly.

Many cars were slipping as I approached State Highway 47, aiming to get gas. Empty tank, yet full bladder. I went around the block once more, to hit a green light, as my car wouldn't have made it up this—most slippery hill of our route—if I sat through the red light, car waiting on the steep incline. Empty tank warning came on, seconds after I strategically made it up that hill. Now needing to pee even more. Bladder starting to scream . . .

Slowly I made it past a few more blocks—craftily weaving up additional ice-covered, slippery hills. Whew. Though two kids in the back had fallen asleep on the way to the gas station, my own breathing was anxious and my body tense. Honestly, not sure at all if my bladder would make it. And, not sure at all if we had enough gasoline fumes to keep the car moving toward the refill, or even home, for that matter.

At last, I pulled into a gas station, with only a couple miles remaining that the car could have puffed out. RELIEF. GRATITUDE. Also, in desperate need of relieving my bladder, I was extra elated to find in this gas station that they had a toilet I could use.

Warm car, napping little ones, finally a full gas tank, and I found a place to pee. Was touch and go there for a while, but God was still so good to me. I started the engine again . . . with such a sense of satisfaction—a deep calm, as though right in that moment I was one of the healthiest or wealthiest grown-ups in the world.

Many people won't understand why this is a story,
or whether there is any point to this story.
Mothers will understand.

Squirrels

What does it say about a person
if they notice squirrels? Some people in the world
hardly know that squirrels exist
while others
will steer the car
around the little creature to save its life.

I used to pay careful attention
to their chewing,
their tiny fingers,
their running,
jumping, chasing,
leaping, courting—

Until
we had our own house
and our own yard in northeast Minneapolis
and the squirrels gained weight, drew near,
walked all over our patio dining table,
ate our spare apples, and
my affection became aversion.

And what, then, does that say about a person?
What does that say about me?

Boughs, willows, breezes, falling leaves.

What have I learned from these, about community?

Trees.

There is a time for social action and a time for reflection.

There is a time for social action and a time for reflection.

There is a time for action . . .

and reflection.

Many quiet, thoughtful people appreciate walking through the trees—to unwind, pray, clear their head. Unfortunately, we generally cannot spend seven days a week, year-round, in contemplation or surrounded by peaceful forests. There are precious children to raise, neighbors to interact with, bills to pay, work projects to finish.

Community is essential. Without interaction, people incline toward mental instability, depression, fearfulness, or greater confusion. But, as we know, relationships are infinitely complex. What do we do, how are we to respond, when these human relationships we invest in can so often inflict wounds or bring pain? Humans intending even to help us might leave one of these marks upon our lives: oppression, cutting criticism, judgments, betrayal, or neglect. Sometimes family or close friends can hit us with all five at once.

Trees are, *at times*, better friends for me than people are. Likely I'm not the only person who's found this to be true. What if, from these trees, which I find so comforting and dependable, I commit to learning something? Yes, I understand this has been done perhaps a hundred times before. I'm not the first person to write about lessons learned from trees. What if I can unravel the metaphor, which trees stand to offer me, for "life in community"?

Beginning with a tree in isolation. If I imagine that a solitary tree represents a middle-aged woman living on her own, in a rural place, what characteristics could I notice, simply in that one tree?

One maple tree generally grows smooth bark when young, and scaly bark when aging. Scaly bark resulting from aging is predestined in the DNA of a maple. This characteristic exists whether the maple stands in a group or stands alone.

A solitary birch tree, while young, has reddish-brown bark, which whitens as the tree matures. The whitening disposition (of any birch) cannot change; the genetic code, its essence, stays consistent. Each tree has its own particular growth journey—involving width, height, depth, bruising, infections, and its own unique way of flexing in the wind. Standing alone, a tree can drip sap, share sap, house birds, or share nuts. It can provide fuel for heating a home or paper for a full class of schoolchildren.

It is the same when a person stands alone. Within each of us is our genetic code, which remains constant as we grow, gives us our eye color, ear for music, inclinations or tendencies when experiencing stress, destined height, broadness of shoulders, our readiness to—or not to—smile big, and our propensity toward forming—or not forming—calluses. A person's unique characteristics and talents can bring only their distinct footprint to influence earth. Only their particular style and sway into the world.

One camphor tree makes a fragrance useful for preserving clothing or deterring insects. While this species exhibits unique qualities, it also *experiences* universal traits. Consider how we read books or watch movies. Our humanity is most touched, most inspired, when we read of or view human experiences shared across the globe. Literature classes might call this "the human experience"; people speaking for the news or another public forum sometimes dub it our "common humanity." Something moves us in our spirit when we are reminded of our commonalities, even while originating from so many different cultures. Alone, one camphor tree makes a fragrance useful for preserving clothes. Yet, at this very moment, camphor trees in Japan, Thailand, Korea, and Vietnam are also busy being camphor trees. Camphor trees doing what camphor trees do—and in four (and more) different nations.

Alone, a walnut tree can be transformed into a fine piece of household furniture and provide nutritious snacks. This walnut tree is an individual, while also pointing to the universal: there are walnut trees in China and in the US, and some from each nation are being used for production of furniture and consumable nuts.

A tree, for many of us, stands to remind us that Jesus died on a cross made of wood and bore all our sicknesses and flaws in his body, so that we may be considered clean. I believe Jesus took a beating so we may be counted forgiven. One person—out of the 7.8 billion other persons currently on earth—views each of us as absolutely acceptable, and He is gazing at us with pure grace, at this moment. He's near us and yet in a realm we cannot see. I can, though, in any tree nearby, rising out of the crumbly soil, see a reminder of that one man.

As individual trees speak to us and nurture us, clusters and groves of trees can also teach us about life. Playing alone can bring a child complete satisfaction, and at other times the isolation brings sadness, irritation, or loneliness. Children playing with other children often send out more and more laughter into the atmosphere.

And if we're to try very hard, we who are grown-ups could remember when forests existed for us as hiding places. For children, trees always have been—and always will be—a fairyland. Trees in a grove may serve as a play house or village. A cluster of trees may represent homes for fairies, vampires, and other unseen friends or foes. Trees can hold shelves, shields, rooms, and glimmering leaves, sheltering vulnerable minds from the sometimes-painful words and paradoxes of the adult realm. Boughs and shadows from groups of trees, then, can speak of mysteries and poems that only children are able to translate—without words.

Eric Rutkow wrote about Verrazzano, the first European to leave a detailed account of a journey to North America. Verrazzano described a particular patch in what is now Maine, marvelling in 1524 that "the wooddes (were) so greate and thicke that an armye . . . mighte have hydd it selfe therein." He labeled her heavily forested land Acadia[1], meaning "idyllic place." (5) Now, this land in Maine is an attractive national park, still serving campers and hikers[2].

One of my favorite things about immersing myself alone in the wilderness, as many moments per year as possible, is the knowledge that there I can stand with no audience save God and myself. If I have talents, I am confident in the wilderness that I'm not acknowledging or using them for the sake of impressing anyone. And as I have flaws (many), no one is nearby to make sure I'm acutely aware of them. In fact, my fears and flaws almost blow off with the wind more quickly when I'm alone than when I am with other people, providing for me a chance of hopeful improvement, providing a very refreshing, open space for my own fresh starts.

A tree never judges a struggling man or woman who seeks a listening ear. Trees simply don't judge. They are who they are, and one can come at them with strength or with flaws. "Come just as you are." A tree is still a tree.

Trees in groups can refresh other trees and other species. To maintain its own sustenance, each tree experiences photosynthesis. Photosynthesis means "to put together with light." Solar energy hits the leaves, causing production of a sugar to feed just that tree. Within this feeding process, oxygen is then released into the air. Trees bless me with oxygen, helping me live and breathe, as a byproduct of their own survival and wellness. What a beautiful image. Along the same vein, when people grow and try to thrive in their own well-being, they offer refreshment and grounding to people in their community.

The world isn't idyllic, though. Trees can harm other trees, as humans can harm other humans, through the spread of illnesses or other toxic influences. Some trees produce fruit or nuts that are harmful when swallowed; conversations involving slander, judgments, and gossip are equally poisonous for people and relationships.

The almond tree grows mainly in California, southwestern Asia, and in Mediterranean climates. Its edible seeds are of two varieties. The sweet almond contains pulp that can be eaten raw, used in cooking, or to form marzipan. Excluding any almond allergy, this almond enhances one who eats it. But the bitter almond: bitter, poisonous, and nonedible in larger quantities. At times, a party or a classroom full of people may revitalize or enrich us, yet other times a contagious virus in one person can send the rest of us home worse off than when we came. Spreadable illnesses, as well as slander, judgment, rude words, or resentments, each spread poison, disease, and sometimes death, to other people.

Rutkow reminds us that almost anywhere a "settler planted an American elm, the tree seemed to thrive. This was part of its charge—it was amongst the hardiest of species. Drought, salt, ice, mild flooding, heavy foot traffic . . . none of it seemed to trouble these unflappable trees" (Rutkow 220, 221). In cities across the United States in the 1800s, thousands of American elms were planted. In the early 1900s, elm sickness went viral across Europe. First, in Holland, Belgium, France, and Germany, these trees began to exhibit browning. Their leaves, branches, and even their root systems changed in color, and would die. In the 1920s, the illness spread to England. By 1930, it was destroying elm trees in east-central parts of the United States, then the plague swept across North America.

A Dutch graduate student discovered the fungus causing the plague (which was carried around from land to land via beetles). Elms in other parts of the world developed a resistance to the fungus. However, when the fungus came on the beetles to the Netherlands, Europe, and North America, these trees did not yet have the vital resistance and died by the millions.

Beetles traveled the globe, and sometimes trees, too, might wind up doing some traveling. What exactly happens when a tree has to move? Trees have been transplanted into new pots, new nurseries, and, at times, even new climates. Sumac trees, orange trees. Cross-cultural marriages, third-culture kids. Many refugee, immigrant, and expat families have experienced a cross-oceanic move and resettled upon a new continent. Our family is right now undergoing such an endeavor on a grand scale. We recently moved from the US Midwest—where we had strong, extensive ties to schools, family, extended family, church communities, and friends—into the heart of Western Europe.

I occasionally need to remind my husband that a wife is more important and more delicate than a potted plant, and must be handled with a lot of extra empathy and care during any transplantation process.

Important questions faced me as I embarked on my own transplantation, into this new ground, especially as I moved with an entire family. How fragile is a child who is taking part in a new school community, immediately after landing overseas? How will a young boy adjust to the new medical system, new dental care, new culture, different humor, and, most importantly, the new mentality regarding friendships? How often should a mother help set up a day and time, or offer a ride, for her son to hang out with a new buddy? Or is it more appropriate to let the young boys make plans regarding timing and transportation entirely without Mom? Among so many other more stressful, more perplexing, questions. And then there's the language barrier.

Mixing nationalities generally enhances all people involved. But sometimes, misunderstandings arise from a collision of cultures or the clash of subcultures. Wrongly reading someone's actions, using our own cultural assumptions to interpret a new friend's behavior, not knowing the best word to articulate a message or to receive a message—these at times can cause real hurts.

Is there something I can learn from Dutch elm disease, as I try to mingle with different cultures, as I cross international borders and connect my heart with many other people? In most circumstances, I've seen God work stunning miracles and create beauty when two or more cultures blend or interact with one another. To encapsulate the path to success in any cross-cultural interchange, from what I have seen and heard, we need just one thing: humility.

Christmas Eve of 1968, William Anders, an astronaut on Apollo 8, took a photo of earth. This was the first picture that human eyes could see of our planet in true form, with pure water lines and tree lines rather than political or map lines. The day after the photo was taken was Christmas Day, and Archibald MacLeish wrote this for the *New York Times*: "To see the earth as it truly is, small and beautiful in that ethereal silence where it floats, is to see ourselves as riders on the earth together, brothers on that bright loveliness in the eternal cold—brothers who know now they are truly brothers."

Political lines and current news headlines do not frequently remind us of our shared brotherhood. Tree lines do.

There is a phrase in the English language, "littered with leaves." In my perspective, leaves are hardly litter. We humans have a vast array of different ways to discard the things that could actually be identified as "treasures."

I've walked through literally thousands of forest trails, in the forty-four years I've been on this planet. In Minnesota, they're called "deer trails." Nearly each deer trail I've hiked has been coated in a layer or two of dead leaves. Normally the word "litter" makes us think of garbage, yet in the woods, waste is only the first half of the story. To be littered with leaves in the forest is to be showered with more than one hundred gifts.

Many people have lately been attempting to "go green," and for good reason. Waste can be recycled. Many vegetable skins could bypass the garbage can and be better used as compost to enliven a garden. Compost replanted in a field for agriculture or stirred into the soil of an orchard creates beauty, new life. God works good things out of our personality conflicts and He transforms the seemingly ugly side of our individual selves into something noble. Personality clashes can be recycled. Every difficulty can be recycled: redemption.

Trees alone and trees in community advise us to try handling our fellow humans with a bit more respect and acceptance. Some personalities are invariable, and everyone's DNA has a significant role to play. Some personalities, or habits of relating, do involve sin issues. Our personal growth can change the atmosphere. Introspection and pruning serve as a photosynthesis to rid the earth and sky of whichever individual habits may be hurting our loved ones, or destroying the community nearby. Perhaps we could all get along better if we laughed more quickly with the beautiful contradiction of you; embraced more often this beautiful, messy me; offered a fiercer type of forgiveness, the sort that rides upon humility; and more willingly and speedily abandoned our own foibles or sins, when these bring obvious pain to others.

Trees breathe life into us. They offer oxygen as well as syrup, nuts, fruits, wood for houses and furniture, and roots preventing land erosion. We lean on trees, find therapy in them, and learn from them that poison and viruses come in a variety of shapes and sizes, from friends and from foes. We can better refresh others when we work on keeping a sound mind and maintaining our own wellness—just as trees share oxygen via their process of being. We can teach future generations the value of humility and the value of looking for the redemption wrapped within the hard things.

Trees teach. Trees produce. Trees help build things. Yet maybe even more profoundly, they are simply here.

Being.

Standing, accepting. Quietly embracing and lovingly listening to you, to me.

1 Trees, rooms, shields, mysteries . . . these are poignant things, touching humans of all ages. Wabanaki people, along with dozens of tribes of First People along the East Coast, had once enjoyed the land and forests of Maine, for thousands of years, while utilizing trees and grasses (birchbark canoes, for example) in thousands of ways. Many Europeans, upon entering this region, required the Wabanaki, and all the First Nations people in the area, to fiercely struggle—simply to dwell on or use their own land. Throughout their resistance, First Peoples displayed incredible power, dedication, hope, and resilience in the face of dehumanizing crimes, colonization, and outsiders' attempts at erasing their hearts, culture, safety, and homes. Only in recent years have these First Nations communities in Maine seen breakthroughs in regaining what was stolen in the 1500s and beyond. Tragically, these breakthroughs are tiny and insufficient, especially considering that children have been stolen away from their parents. Breakthroughs barely to be classified as breakthroughs. The road to recovery (as with each realm of injustice still existing in America today) demands attention, awareness, and involvement from each one of us.

2 The formation of this national park was a story of injustice. To repair, return, or make things right will be a complicated journey and we've all only just begun. The justice and rightness is starting more slowly than First Peoples need, but it has to start; anyone living in the US lives on land that once belonged to First Nation communities, and yet we all have a God-given thirst to hike or swim or meander through nature, somehow. Ojibwe and Dakota lived first, before my family, in the spaces where I spent my childhood. At the very least, when we do hike, dwell, swim, or meander, we can be first repentant (over the ways our federal system and our own subconscious mentalities have been oppressing people, in various means yet unknown by almost all of us, as Americans), and secondly, we can be grateful. Much more to say about increasing justice, and resisting structural racism, trauma, and injustice in this land. But this cannot be explored to its completion, in *Half Moon Waking*. The rightness, justice, and repentance will be complicated and confusing, but it's a path that we must still enter into, and move humbly forward with open ears and open hearts. More and more books need to be written (better said, to be *read*) by all of us, in the raising up of repair, and true shalom.

As we hike on American soil, we can start exercising baby steps of social justice by simply being aware (mindful) of the scars these First Nations communities carry, scars from every single unfair battle endured.

Three Does in an Oak Grove

the purity of the sensual

      is free

it is the dignity of beige-brown wilderness

unashamed of its power

      unashamed of rough-edge bark

and humble in its tear-wrenching austerity

the purity of the sensual

                                        is instinct

three does

in an oak grove

standing so warm-near to one another

      guile less

      un envious

restless

not because they feel unwelcome or un-enticing

                but because their brownbrain

                in the cold northwoods

                tells them simply when to focus

or when to flee

Do you remember junior high? Most of us probably could swap some intensely embarrassing moments, and most of us remember avoiding crowds whenever possible. Every town had nature somewhere near—near enough to reach. You remember, right? That most of you chose to spend more summer hours (of that uncertain and shaky season) so much closer to the wild than to any gathering of classmates—other kids whose personal self-doubts and insecurities were (of course) dumped upon you, via projection or exclusion, in ways only adolescents can really pull off? When I was in junior high, one of my sisters and I wished intensely to swim in the river not far from our house. It ran by, each summer day, with its natural beauty; warm, brown . . . *fun*. Mom had concerns about the current and our safety. She said we couldn't swim there until we reached a certain level in our swimming lessons. Finally, one summer during early middle school, we finished the Advanced Swimmers class at the Fergus Falls YMCA, and our wait was over!

Running through tall prairie grass to the Ottertail River, and canoeing a small bit south, we gleefully abandoned our life jackets on the green, cattail island, and swam in the shallow places and the deep. The rush of a somersault in the warm, brown water, the blinding sparkle of sunlight on the surface, the cool wind skipping toward our faces—all felt incredibly good: bright sun yielding empowerment to me; wild wind communicating freedom. And the knowledge that we were being trusted on an adventure requiring caution, care, and capability made us feel strong, maturing, hope-filled.

Also through our early middle school years, our family began to buy and ride horses. I was so excited, learning how to feed and care for them, and especially learning to ride. I've been aware that this is a rare opportunity, and that many little girls would have wished to own a horse. Even today, I am humbled and so grateful to have been given that chance.

When the riding lessons began, the focus was on a whole lot of walking and a bit of trotting, yet I yearned for the day when I could *canter* (a slow gallop). Dad said that since Bunny was our gentlest, safest horse, she would be the one I could first canter on. After waiting many months for Dad to take me out with Bunny, the long-awaited moment came. I had the privilege of loping Bunny along a highway ditch and near the green, sun-kissed farm fields just outside of my hometown.

After waiting and waiting, a rocking horse was beneath me while her three-beat patterns sounded in my ears. So many glad butterflies flew in my chest, and I knew my kind-hearted dad was watching over me from the horizon. I was soaring, and my soul was extremely thankful.

Psalm 27:14 relays David's source of hope, as he waited for God to deliver him from his pursuers (aka attackers). "Wait for the Lord; be strong and take heart and wait for the Lord." Waiting often can be a time of questioning, unknowns, or blindness.

Like David, other psalmists wrote about waiting for the Lord during times of suffering, including the words of Psalm 43 and Psalm 77. Psalm 130, in verses five and six, states, "I wait for the Lord, my soul waits, and in His word I put my hope. My soul waits for the Lord more than watchmen wait for the morning, more than watchmen wait for the morning." Again, a poem and a plea written by David.

With the Lord, a thousand years are like a day. From His perspective, humans are clay on His pottery wheel. Compared to the Creator, we are so small and weak, and when we ask Him to move, advise, or provide, our requests may be so far off the mark from what we truly need or what will more deeply satisfy. God has every right to take His time responding to our "tiny" cries, though He never views our needs or our cries as "tiny." He sees many people on this small earth who are undergoing very large traumas. He sees the very real hurts taking place. God sees and He cares—about our little concerns as well as our gigantic struggles.

And while He often has His own mysterious time frame in the responding, *we wait*.

During my semester abroad in a remote valley of West Papua, part of Indonesia, I learned a lot about waiting. My seven female classmates and I regularly waited our turn for the one shower. Many of us were in a challenging life season, waiting for clarity in our career or next job steps, hoping for . . . someday . . . a life partner, a husband. And with the employees of the local post office so frequently *istirahat* (resting), we waited for days—sometimes weeks—to send out our communications. Due to some government corruption and departmental inefficiency in our region, we generally waited a month before we received response mail . . . or any words from home. We couldn't access emails, as our location was so remote. We consequently underwent weeks: wondering what was going on at home, what loved ones were thinking, or what our close friends felt about our last letter. Through that waiting . . . I was pressed to notice more about the personalities of the young men and women near me, and to depend more upon the potential new friends living with me. Through that waiting . . . I was also forced to hear from God in the silence rather than seeking answers from those at home. And through that waiting, the letter felt so good, once it was finally in my hand. The long-anticipated words were profound, heavy with value.

My college roommates in St. Paul, Minnesota, came up with the term "actively wait." What a beautiful idea. I guess it's somewhat like "active listening," yet with less pressure on another person—more of a self-check. We're free to "do things" while we wait for answers from God. Often "other things" than working toward our anticipated result. We can allow God to use us even during the times we feel weakened by uncertainty or doubts. And we can learn something. When God is silent on one subject, we can be intentional to discover what else He would have us learn about ourselves or about Him.

Revising this essay as an early middle-aged wife and mother: I'm (slowly) seeing that the most beautiful treasures in life are those that involve pain, time, and great effort. I am more aware of the cries and needs of people around me, and I'm more grateful when I at last can find the answers: the safe delivery of my child, straightening a crucial relationship that had become warped, healthier dynamics in my marriage.

And about this marriage, I've been learning that there are things to continue praying for and asking God to change in self or my spouse, especially when certain behaviors are hurting one of us, or damaging our friendship. As I'm waiting on God, I already know the actions He wants me to take (and I should laugh here, but it's really not that easy): remove the planks from my own eye, grow in my own areas of weakness, increase my ability to self-soothe, pursue what brings me joy, worship Jesus in spite of troubles, and increase my own level of differentiation.

We all wait. Career moves, healing of a scary illness, waiting for someone to approach us or interact with us in healthier ways, or waiting for someone to forgive us. Many of us are wondering why God has not successfully stopped Putin from invading and traumatizing the people of Ukraine (whether via miracles or through his use of people in the positions of law enforcement or human rights). Many of us wait for God to send some more *visible* angels, to rescue cities of Syria from any further bombing or devastation. We all want to ask, *Why should it take this long, God?! If you are so real, and if you care at all?!*

Even when we don't see the purpose for the delays, I believe God does see, and does have a purpose for our waiting on tangible gifts in this life, as well as for the intangibles. Over the upcoming thousands of years, date unknown, many of us must wait for the consummation of the Kingdom, Christ's second coming, our transformation into Christ-like-ness, among many other spiritual realities. Romans 8:23 says, "We . . . who have the firstfruits of the Spirit, groan inwardly as we wait eagerly for our adoption as sons [and daughters], the redemption of our bodies." And I think that while we're waiting for God to *really* move, save, to work His rescue operations, we continue to pray. We keep on doing everything that is in our means to empower and encourage people near to us or far. We do what we can, when we can, to restore the earth, to rebuild people. Doing nothing isn't one of the helpful choices.

Waiting for Him flips our weakness into His strength, can flip our younger decades into a lot of fun even while we experience graceful maturity. Working inside His timing helps us to develop and expand, yet in such a way that we retain the joy of living and can still taste freedom. Waiting for Him helps us to notice the people, needs, or resources standing directly in front of us. Patiently waiting for Him builds our dependence on Him . . . until we finally see that the crisp, colorful map is already secure in Jesus' hands. Waiting for Him snatches the control away from us: The sun and water wink wildly, amused by our manipulations and fears, ready to remind us that the Creator sees and knows a whole lot. (Waiting in itself *is* a fierce adventure.) And waiting for Him turns our knee-jerk cravings, assumed needs,* or our gigantic questions into *even bigger* blessings flowing from His wisdom—blessings perfectly shaped and fitted for the right moment.

* Syria and Ukraine were mentioned in this essay not to minimize their struggles, but rather to ensure that I draw attention to them, to highlight and emphasize the need to pray for them. It's important to me that Syria's and Ukraine's situations are considered, and are covered in more and more prayers, even as the book is going through its final drafts. By no means do I believe or suggest that wishing for war to end is a "knee-jerk craving" or "an assumed need." Only that this particular essay was first written long before 2014, and is filled with mixtures: examples of horrendous waiting seasons as well as examples of simple personal needs and wants, not yet realized.

and then there were five

two healthy oranges on one young tree

plus five potential sunflower faces in the same orchard

encircling their own bright pollens

and wishes come to faces

Inside of Still

inside of stillness
a seed does in fact feel something
feeling the pressure

of the full weight of peace
in every wave of quietness and rest
there are still beams

        sun and light energy
still moving

and these move toward me to take hold of my core
while they also hold my hand

        lovingly

they gently walk me to forgotten old homes inside

        and carefully lead me into a new relationship with all of you

Still Walking I

It's a round earth, not a flat earth.

Living in the here and now with conflicts—
one permanent relationship tying a confusing equator

round the lover and the discord.

Still Walking II

Still feeling the shock waves of the lonelier nights in my hemisphere
—after evenings unresolved.

If we fight, we have both lost.

Cleverness, rightness, wisdom cannot bridge the

divide

between two persons who have already become one
and then

separate. A hole—

Still Walking III

A whole. Dark night, boring a hole through earth's infinitely circular core

yet people on the other side are still going to work. What—
they just pretend, during evenings like these? Is that even genuine? Sincere?

But it is morning there.

The people are walking upside down because it's day there and yes, husband and wife are
still married. Happily.

Their heads hang in carefree oblivion below their street shoes and even below their briefcases.
The moment my heart is painted with pain and left unresolved, their sun is shining and they are
still going to work
on their upside-down trains, even their upside-down sidewalks.

Still walking.

"I'm a songwriter, and this is my song for today. This song may never make it 'big,' but I am a songwriter and this is simply my song for today. This is just who I am, and this is what I do . . . " a woman said during a radio interview, as she concluded her description of a folksy song she'd just played.

The canvas of life provides so many unique motivations for our work. Some jobs are trades, crafts which we've been trained in, specified roles that (hopefully) help pay the bills. We often head to work out of a sense of responsibility, to provide income. There is also work which helps us feel satisfied and alive; some call these hobbies, some call them outreach or ministry. (Still others are lucky enough to say "I have a job that I absolutely love!") When we think about discovering our destiny, finding a career that we find fulfilling, or sorting out our calling, we're not "only" trying to arrange our bliss. We're also not "merely" punching the time clock to make ends meet. We each have before us an entire scale of soul-motivations. Grown-ups could be having a lot more fun if only we'd believe that we get to create our own life-mixture of many of these elements, no matter how many hours may already be demanded to balance the budget.

My family made periodic road trips to Alberta, Canada to visit loved ones when we lived in Minnesota, US. Sometimes I was a professional writer, seated shotgun in the big minivan, scribbling poems and writing in a notebook. At other times I was the pilot of our large craft, soaring over the tar highways. Yet during many other minutes I served as a hospitality coordinator: planning our next campsite or hotel. For many other hours, I held the simple responsibility of scouting out the next gas station. And other hours, I was responsible for entertaining our toddler travelers in creative ways. All roles were important.

A funny thing about motherhood is that we wear so many different hats, each day. We're constantly in caregiver mode, often a nurse, sometimes a doctor, eternally a teacher, and many of us are assigned thousands of hours of cooking assignments per year. Often, as the kids grow older, the mother's routine changes, her job description is rewritten, and options for other paid employment become more spacious.

Our callings are also impacted greatly by the nuances of marriage.

So many of us search out our *calling*. During those unsteady seasons when it's tricky to discern, I've loved the concept spelled out in the book of John: "Remain in me and I will remain in you" (15:4). Life and fruitfulness (productivity?) are about keeping close company with the invisible

Jesus, made visible in the pages of the Bible.

In my work with a wholistic community development organization, from 2002 until 2006, we often described together (through our study of the Bible) the primary calling for all Christ-followers as loving God. Secondary calling: love thy neighbor.

One night, while I was still an active part of this ministry and development team, I was lying in bed, not yet asleep, and God brought a Scripture reference to my mind. I had never memorized the words in that chapter, but the voice was clearly speaking to me. *Isaiah 43*. I felt compelled finally to roll over, turn on the light, and pick up the Bible:

But now, this is what the LORD says—he who created you, O Jacob, he who formed you, O Israel: "Do not be afraid, for I am with you; I will bring your children from the east and gather you from the west . . . and my daughters from the ends of the earth—everyone who is called by my name, whom I created for my glory, whom I formed and made. . . . You are my witnesses . . . and my servant whom I have chosen, so that you may know and believe me and understand that I am He. Before me no god was formed, nor will there be one after me. . . . No one can deliver out of my hand. When I act, who can reverse it? . . . See, I am doing a new thing! Now it springs up; do you not perceive it? . . . I am making a way in the wilderness and streams in the wasteland . . . to give drink to my people, my chosen . . . the people I formed for myself . . . that they may proclaim my praise."

I was blown away by God's reality and God's voice as He spoke that night. God's heartbeat is "missions" and He is completely capable of wooing more and more people into a closer connection with Himself. He sees when a sparrow falls, He desires the hungry to find food, He desires broken hearts to be healed, and He desires His shalom and His restoration to be realized. Part of our responsibility as humans is to simply watch—to stand in wonder at His reality. He is taking care of it *all*. God has living energy and He does things—things He could easily do without us. How silly we are whenever we forget this. Yet, how privileged we are, that the Creator still invites us to play a part in fighting oppression, alleviating poverty, and befriending the outcasts, among so many other ways we're able to get involved in this healing process.

"Stay in your lane" is a phrase with apparently many meanings and many uses in the United States. However, when it comes to my calling, your calling, everyone's callings, it's helpful to remember to stay in our lane. Competition and insecurity become nonissues if we have a clear understanding of what we are called to do each day. Instead of looking around or questioning how our roles or tasks compare to someone else's, we're able to have peace and happiness fixing our attention on that Audience of One. When we can be or do what our Father in Heaven is asking us to be or do each day, when we know we are making our Creator smile with pleasure, pride, or gratitude for the attitude in our hearts, the other demands and pressures are defunct.

We've all been named human beings, not human doings. This reflects Jesus' clarification, "The Kindgom of Heaven is within you" (Luke 17:21 MEV). Real joy comes from internal and not external factors. Real love and real kindness flow first from genuine affection in the heart; while the visible acts of serving someone, doing chores, or helping a neighbor might not necessarily be loving—if they're lacking authenticity. Could be helpful, yes; but an expression of love, often not. A human being is existing, first. Kindness is way more refreshing to those around us when there is real fondness within our own heart.

The Kingdom of Heaven is existing, first. The Kingdom of Heaven never pushes too hard, and it wouldn't allow a sense of striving or overexertion to smash the soft spots or extinguish the attachments felt between two people.

"Abide in me," (John 15:4 ESV).

"Apart from me you can do nothing," Jesus said (John 15:5).

Jesus Christ wants to be the bread we eat. Christ defines Himself as a source, analogous to a power cord providing energy for His disciples' serving, loving, or our working. When we sorta notice ourselves striving—toward anything—we may have drifted from the central love affair. This loving relationship, involving constant communication between Jesus and ourselves, is a gift for us: while we work in the factory, while we work in an office, while we preach, while we wash the dishes, while we teach a child. This joyful love, from heaven to us and from us to those near us, provides fuel—gives direction for all our tasks. Living inside Him and making space for Him to live inside us.

I do believe there are certain callings, jobs, and roles that are written into some people's hearts and will be useful at some points during our lives. Many individuals are simply not well-suited to be a phys-ed teacher, many are not wired for the role of CEO, and others feel clumsy with accounting. Still others are uncomfortable working full-time with papers, grammar, websites, or words.

In a given week, my husband and I have completed plenty of work hours that have not provided income, and plenty of work hours that have. This palette of choices exists, from which we all could plan our schedule, while also remembering to safeguard time each year for the activities in which our talents lie. There's something inspiring and healing in our minds and souls, whenever we spend time fully lost (abandoned!) within some form of creative process or activity that we *genuinely* enjoy. We all frequently encounter fuzzy areas, or some blending of roles, when we operate in our families, in our places of employment, or in our church bodies.

However, in every one of these spaces, I think we can first stay close to Jesus each day, and we will then find occasional outlets to serve—even at times within the areas of our talents or interests. We're always surrounded by people who are hurting, people in need of nurturing. Some days it might be our selves. Often, we need to strengthen our own mind, body, or heart via the nurturing or creative solutions that God provides.

I believe staying close to Jesus is the clearest job description we've been given for today. Tomorrow will bring its own assortment of choices, colors, dimensions, and directions, and we are—we will be—human beings loving.

A FICTION STORY

Panting and exhausted, the two young boys reached the top of the hill they called the Mountain of the Kings. As soon as their scanty suppers were over, it was their tradition to meet outside the stone walls of their town, run to the top of this expansive slope, and take their thrones above the vast domain of Ireland's melancholy beauty. Sweat trickled unchecked down Micah's olive-colored face, and Kyle's freckled face wore a determined yet happy grimace. They both tackled the crest of the steep, green "mountain" neck and neck.

Kyle and Micah collapsed in a loud chorus of breathing and heavy sighing, spreading their arms out wide to allow heaving lungs to take in as much air as possible. They didn't need to congratulate each other on reaching the summit. All Kyle had to do was extend a hand to carelessly pat his friend on the chest. They had made it.

The autumn breeze from the North Atlantic Ocean careened over the slopes. It picked up speed while chasing the boys' shadows up the great hill, tousling their hair, refreshing their faces. Grey clouds were coasting toward them from the sea, hovering close to the ground, occasionally hiding the sun and giving the boys a chill.

Out of the corners of their eyes, the boys saw wildflowers tilting.

"I see a little Norman activity down in the corner of that valley, sir," Micah began the drama. A handful of lambs had trotted toward their mothers.

"We'll release a few good men down there, then. We'll have them ride around the far side of that slope and attack them from behind those trees there." Kyle played right along.

These two kings, the first in history to actually share one title, one territory, sat proudly on their grassy thrones, surveying *their* kingdom. Green fields and hills were dotted with scattered grey stones.

The blob of white dots, which was a small sheep herd, walked a couple of steps closer to the stream, way down in the valley, toward greener grass. "It looks like we may need to hire more Scottish mercenaries," Micah declared ominously.

"Yes, sir. Let's get them before they get us," Kyle said. Every evening, all it took was a wandering sheep or a flock of birds to trigger their theatrics. They hadn't yet spied any real Normans. But over lunch, their apprenticeship masters would relate the news that they had heard in town, of Norman activity in Dublin or Leinster, and these stories would fuel adventures taking place in the boys' minds on top of the Mountain of the Kings.

After a couple of hours dispatching soldiers and strategizing attacks, the boys turned west again to make their way down their little mountain, their great hill. The sun was sinking low along the horizon, over the Atlantic, and they knew their masters would want them in at a decent hour. They picked their way over large rocks and slid down the rubble of tiny grey pebbles.

"At my apprenticeship today I did finally stick something in the fire!" Micah said. "Mr. Flendike did let me hold a couple horseshoes in the blue flame to reshape them. He's finally trusting me."

"Really? I am still only watching Mr. Hobson's work. Today it was sanding chairs. I thought he could have let me help him. I don't expect to carve chair legs yet, but sanding, that I could do . . . ."

"Yeah . . . . You should have seen the way that blue flame melts the metal. It's like watching ice melt!"

Near the bottom of the hill they parted ways, each sneaking into town from different gates in the stone wall. Micah jogged to the north end, the Jewish section, and Kyle to the south, the Christian section.

❧❧❦

Shoulders broadened and the pals grew beards. Micah, a thick, brown beard; Kyle with a thin, red beard. Finally, Micah could do some of the finer shaping and harder work with Mr. Flendike, and Kyle could do more than merely fetching mallets—or watching.

Occasionally, Micah would show up at Kyle's apprenticeship with a basket lunch for them to share. Kyle would tell his master that it was a friend from church. Mr. Hobson would grunt and continue pounding nails or sanding, sending up sawdust.

During lunch breaks together, the two teenagers would share stories of attractive young women who walked past their shops.

Kyle laughed one day and threw back his head. "What do you do when you catch them staring?"

"I just look up with a suave smile and say 'Good day, ladies.'"

"Yeah, me too. Then I roll up my sleeves so they can get a better look at my arms, when they do walk by a second time!" They both laughed again.

❧❧❦

Another chilly autumn day, and Kyle's family was surrounding the dinner table after their Sunday Mass. One of Kyle's three sisters had just sat down after pouring water for each clay drinking mug. They all bowed their heads in prayer.

"Great God in Heaven, please look down in mercy on us. Give us our daily bread. Keep us safe from the black death. Amen." Kyle's father began cutting open his potato.

"What's this?" Kyle asked.

"Plague."

"What 'plague'?"

"It's coming from the Continent. Terrible now. Wiping out great cities and even countries! One of my customers kennen one who's been struck."

"Did it start in the north end of town?" Mama asked. "I'm certain it did. Those Jews will bring their own curse upon us. You, you children must stay away from the Jews! Do you understand?" Kyle and his three sisters nodded. "And, you hear of a Jew being struck, you may be certain it is God's right wrath punishing him. If you hear of a Christian being struck, you may be so sure that some evil Jew had poisoned the well! And may God's will be done!"

Father chewed slowly, so heavy in thought that he didn't look at Mama as she spoke.

Early the next morning, as Kyle walked to Hobson's shop, he saw two old, stooped women on the street, swapping their local "news." He heard one say to the other, "The dirty creatures, where did they come from? Infecting us with their curse . . . " Both women crossed themselves.

He passed a man selling fish. "This one?" The purchaser nodded. "You know anyone been struck?"

Two girls walked up behind Kyle, arms hooked. He caught their conversation. "Mama tells me that it's because the Jews poison the wells . . . . "

At the shop, those words, "God's will be done," echoed through his head as he pounded nails. *What is so bad about the Jews? Micah is the best friend I've ever known.* Mr. Hobson pointed out the fine decorative pattern on the legs of a chair, to a customer. "Yes, this was crafted by Kyle here. Good hands, he has."

The vehemence with which his mother spoke penetrated into his heart. "Or are you looking for something simpler? We have that, too. Please, look here." Hobson led the customer across the little workshop. *God is a sovereign God. He must have a reason for sending us the plague. Perhaps it is the Jews' fault?* Kyle's hands moved automatically over the grey nails he had pounded in. *God's will be done. God's will be done.*

Later, as the sun settled high in the sky, Kyle waited for Micah to stop in to share a lunch. But Micah, the forbidden friend, did not come. A fleeting fear crossed his mind. *Was Micah taken with the plague? Does he deserve the plague?*

For the first time, Kyle considered Micah almost someone to . . . to avoid.

Kyle pulled on a coat that evening, and began walking to the Jewish end of town. Finally, he reached the blacksmith's shop. Stepping inside the dark interior, Kyle looked at the vacant fire pit in the center of the room. Lining the walls of the small shop were tables covered with orderly rows of heavy tools, blackened from their hours in the fire. Mr. Flendike's residence was upstairs. Young apprentices also boarded there during their training. Kyle walked—nervous—through the dark little shop, and firmly knocked on a thick, black door near the back.

Mr. Klendike answered. "Sick man in the house," he said softly and began to shut the door. Kyle placed his foot between the door and the jamb.

"Is it Micah? I'm his best friend. I need to see him," he said.

"You want to put your life in danger?"

Kyle remembered his mother's words. *God's will be done.*

"I need to see him," Kyle insisted.

The old man nodded and opened the door. They trudged up the narrow stairway, to the attic, an attic which several apprentices over the years had once called home, during their own season of schooling.

Suffering is because of a sin you committed. Suffering is God's way of making you a better person.

In a far corner, Micah lay on a thin mattress. His fingers and nose were black and his body shook with perilous, overwhelming chills. Black tumors the size of chicken eggs protruded from his skin. Kyle stared at his friend, wishing he himself was not in a Christian family, wishing Micah was not a Jew. Kyle stared, wishing he didn't have to wonder if he was supposed to hate his friend, change him, or forget him.

A woman leaned over Micah. Tears streamed down her cheeks as she stroked his hair.

The woman, who appeared to be Micah's mother, looked at Kyle. Pain distorted her face. Her tears immediately melted Kyle's heart, a heart congested with so many questions.

He walked swiftly to the bed and knelt across from Micah's mother. Micah opened his mouth as soon as he recognized Kyle.

"Don't, Micah! Rest . . . Shhhhh." His mother wept louder.

The words came out slowly and slurred. "Ye . . . you keep those . . . N-Normans . . . back . . . alright?" Kyle nodded. There was a long, tense pause, as Micah struggled for the strength again to speak. "S-send the Scot-Scot—ish . . . merc . . . ye have to . . . a . . . right?" Kyle nodded, unable to speak, his throat feeling full and constricted. Tears filled his eyes.

The eyes of Micah's mother glistened, tears refracting in the candlelight. Slowly a realization lit up her features, and she looked at Kyle intently.

"Don't go," Kyle whispered to Micah.

"I'll . . . I'll tell God . . . send you sweet . . . wind over our . . . our mountain, and . . . and to give . . . give you . . . vic-victory in battle."

Micah's mother took Kyle's hand in hers. He smiled knowingly at the grieving woman, who had a new light in her eyes, and she smiled back.

Before the sun had fully cleared Ireland's mountains the next morning, or attained the west-facing slopes, Kyle was slowly trudging up the Mountain of the Kings, alone. With every step, the words ran through his mind, *God's will be done, God's will be done.*

When he reached the top, he fell to his knees. Lifting his eyes toward the sky, where pink clouds were expanding left and right, making way for larger sun, he prayed aloud. "Our Father, which art in Heaven, hallowed be Thy name. Thy kingdom come, Thy will be done—"

Kingdom come. "Thank You . . . for friendship. Thank You for the wonder of having a friend—such a *good* friend. Thy kingdom is . . . has . . . already been here." He quietly laughed.

Friendship

(the English version)

by Walter Hunziker

To hate, one most have loved.
To search, one must have asked,
"Is there something missing here?"
Friendship will be
as raindrops from above,
wetting those streams which trickle past.
Friendship will nurture grace-filled fields,
guarding against
even
barrenness.

In life, we all ask, "How much pain can I endure?"
No more, no less.
Maybe only as much as the rain we have allowed to fall
on us.
Friendship will be
as money invested well.
As the parable of the talents, buried befriending will bring nothing,
while the investing of the few that we do grasp . . .
will bring . . .
more in fact. When we feel at our lowest
and we know we are nothing, have nothing,
the life and the rain must still be spent,
shared, dropped, invested.

Friendship does not grow on trees
after all.
Live well, endure long.
Reach out to more than one hand.
Sorrow is certain to visit,
but its shadow will fade with the relieving presence
of yet another grateful friend.

Friendship

     (the Schweizer-Deutsch version)

     by Walter Hunziker

Um Eim z'hasse, müsst Eim au scho g'liebt ha.

Um Öppis z'süche, müsste Eim scho bewusst sie das Öppis fählt.

Fründschaft wird wie erfrischende Räggetröpf von Himmu,

Sie netzt d' Bächli das waltzt verbie.

Fründschaft wird Gnad g'füllt Felder ernähre

und schutzt vor das leere Wüste.

Im lauf von Läbe, frage Ig mir,

"wie veu Leide kann Ig verliede?"

Nid meh, nid weniger, als d' Menge vo Räggetröpf das mir verschänke.

Fründschaft isch wie Gäwd, gut investiert;

wie im G'schicht von vergrabene Talent wird "vergrabene Befreundig" au nüt bringt,

aber herz-vollem investieren im Fründschaft bringt organisch Wachstum!

Wenn mir fülle üus am Ände, mit nüt meh zum gä—

das Läbe und Rägge muss immer-noh spendiert, g'teult . . . investiert.

Fründschaft wachst haut nid uf d'Bäum,

lebt grossartig, haute durch!

Streck ües mehr als ei Hand,

Leide werde Üus ganz sicher b'süche,

aber siem Schate wird vergo im heilende Pressänz vo

no an'andere dankbare Früend.

What Is Real?

In the silence of early dawn, the bells toll in two hemispheres. The Dani women quietly spread out into the sweet potato fields of West Papua, as the Minnesota mothers in the framed churches guide their sons and daughters into chairs. The sun sends a flood of light at a long angle, pouring over the mountain tops and trickling into the nooks and crannies of Great Baliem Valley. Pools of morning sun rest on the heads of Katina and Ilena. Gleams of Sunday sun, on the other side of earth, stream through stained-glass windows to cheer the seated participants of morning worship. The lime-green grass and yellow mountaintop are the soul and breath of the scene.

We stride barefoot to the dark *ubi** ground. And back at the fire pit, Dani men use their pronged forks to lift stones onto the fire just as Texan men in the church elder-board meeting bow their heads to lift up the community in prayer. Men chant in time with a drum beat. The stones sizzle in the smoke; gossip, no doubt, sizzles in the ladies' room, while we kneel in the soil to dig through the ubi greens. We search until we find the body of a real live sweet potato. We dig for the real thing, as biblical scholars, on every continent, dig for real answers to make real live curricula.

And we all smile silently and humbly together when we know we've found

The Real Thing.

* *ubi* is the Bahasa Indonesian word for sweet potato

Beauty, Part I
        (written as single, young woman in university)

And it was like two men in Passima village, holding hands,
orange flowers situated in their hair.
And Grannie and Gramps sitting humbly side by side, she in her silk, off-white robe, he in his
red pajamas—
stoic,
watching the evening news and blonde reporter,
while headlines
        and white captions
                        strolled across the screen.

It felt like an unexpected, unrequested reunion,
or the bitterness of betrayal becoming now an open door,

like the sparkle in a healthy baby's gaping brown eyes.
Like the reaching, kicking strides of a Kenyan runner
pounding upon his orange and neon-green shoes,

and the shiny, black hair of a child.
It was as beautiful as the moment brunette twins discovered a difference,
beautiful as a sister's strange warning.

Like the wet wind and clouds blowing
over aged, rocky crags.
Like a mystery that only becomes more unclear with time,
a sad kiss on the cheek, a brisk kiss on the forehead.

It was my cousin's crumb-filled, four-year-old kiss,
like tears in the brown, frowning eyes
of a lonely, old dog.

It was a forgotten language
returning to the tongue.

Like the rain falling and the sun shining at the same time.

Beauty, Part II
            (written in early middle age, as mother, as wife)

And it is like the blue-brown energy
in my husband's sea-deep eyes when he remembers

to allow other people's needs, other people's admiration,
                                                    to drift into his background,
and to really look toward me

            with his entire heart.
                            —as though I have startled him   —with reality   —with a gift.

Like the elderly couples who sit at restaurants and
don't need to talk.
It is like my daughter's readiness to smile, or my son's incredibly searching thoughts, or all
of our questions
when mixed well together.

As lovely as a neighbor who tries to flash a smile more often than not,
even when life is not

easy.

As beautiful as the grandparents
trusting the parents
                    . . . a little . . . bit . . . more,

and
it is as welcoming as the warm, round eyes of a swiss dairy cow
as she's relaxing near the fence. I bike past.
Beautiful

as our own sweet parents and in-laws
seeing a little more clearly
how deeply we desire a good friendship
with them,

like the warm calm that bathes . . .
            the hopeful butterflies that immerse . . . my lungs and my heart
                        to a condition beyond tranquility

the moment I smell
and breathe in smoke

from a wood-burning stove nearby.

Shhhhhhh

With the hush of an immigrant settling in,
the peace finds deep, new calm.
Snow off the roof blows the trees blows the wind
'til
free to laugh, it quiets down.

Rocking, the tree tops groan under peace
so strange, so wise, so thick.
The profundity shames the roaring truck;
silence crushes the clock.

"I've forgotten you," we have to say,
humbly, and out loud,
as the truth comes crashing down to us
with Resurrection Pow'r.

Snow off the roof blows the trees blows the wind
'til
free to laugh, it settles down.
Snow off the roof blows the clouds blows the drifts
blows the clouds to another town.

Peace frowns with new reflection
and sits heavily on a tree;
seeps into our window with the promise
that it's okay to sleep.

nearly where blueberries grow
two old men tip a clay pitcher and
water
cool with youth
covers the mug floors

cleansing
teaching   completing
the blue-grey ceramic emptiness

and cider still reaches into their memory

white eyelashes (cough)
and skiing all of Saturday   where brown cocoa spilled on grey farming mittens
where (cough) boiling water was impressionably blue under dusk's summerlike eyes

where rattling days and
blue-grey shadows
both die once

and evening walks into the door

a small bell rings

our hearts cannot contain this joy

Light Wood

Light flows even out of no light.

Wood upholds this notebook and the notebook itself
is made of shredded wood dust.
Every page of every book was once wood in an earlier life. Lighter light . . .

light being.

Now may we share coffee over the table and speak softly of our hearts.
Sure we can find something to laugh about . . .
as life is hardening, freezing. See the wood on the floor, against the wall,
        or within the tabletop.
There is a light that doesn't run low
and wood is always here. Softly
still glowing.

When I was four, butterflies—the happy kind—often filled my gut. I wandered bright-eyed through my mornings and afternoons (and sometimes nights). My thoughts stretched wider than the green front yard, and the whole year brimmed with existential questions. Around me lay life itself: my family, a playroom, a planet, and, of course, our front yard full of possibilities. With a sister or a friend, I played make-believe nearly daily. It was easier for me then, when life was fun and games, to believe in an unseen realm and a caring Deity. I'm not sure why, but I asked a lot of philosophical questions that year, according to many of my relatives.

Fun times and big dreams. Later, approaching adulthood. The decades between ages fourteen and thirty-four brought me some intense encounters with disillusionment and the disintegration of more than a small handful of certain wishes, visions, dreams.

However! My days of early adulthood also provided more treasures, cooler relationships, and greater experiences than I'd even thought to hope for. God's existence, our faith in Him, cause for optimism, the expectation of good things; are these only feasible for us when we're young, innocent, and free of burdens?

Before my son and daughter entered my life, I had honestly anticipated that my four-year-old's inquiries, as we walked hand in hand, would teach me more about God's truth or goodness. (Their wisdom floating in on whispers and animal cracker breath.) Enter the Kingdom of Heaven like a child, right?

Yet, toddlers in the family, mixed with walking, mixed with faith . . . actually bring limited—sparse—opportunities for carefree fun, with hardly any peaceful gardens, or answers, or strolls.

I now know.

The battle to be gentle, rational, or kind, while sleep-deprived, commenced as soon as the first baby spent their first night at home. The combination: of faith, of walking through a day (or night) of family togetherness, and of raising children, meant recovering sometimes from severe, labor-tearing-perineum-pain, additional marital strife, and a stomach stretching past the point of no return.

But, as I understand it today, that which most separates actual parenthood from faith, imaginative optimism, and creative fun in the front yard is namely doubt.

Doubt.

Even before I became Mommy, doubt was just as much a reality, in my own mind and heart, as faith was. Some mornings, heading into another day as a single woman, I held a real belief in God. I knew for sure that Jesus could save us all. I often leaned on God, as a single woman, and I was usually certain He listened carefully when I spoke to Him. Yet other mornings I simply wasn't certain God was a person nearby, or that God cared about my struggles or joys. And it was okay to have those days, sort of, when it was just me, no kids.

But, that was before. . . .

The spiritual journey becomes a bit muddled when I want to impart the good news, or any beliefs about God, to an inquisitive toddler. Or is that really what I want to teach my kids after all?

As I take a big breath today, a reality wants to sit on my shoulders like a burp cloth smelling of milk. Again, Heaven wants to remind me: the toddler and child exist primarily to teach me about the Kingdom of Heaven. And that, after all, is what my heart was wishing for . . . originally . . . before I first held someone in my womb. The surprising element is this: the *learning* is via the *listening* to their *questioning*. What have my (now) fourteen-year-old and eleven-year-old taught me, thus far?

My son frequently asked me, when he was three or four, "Where is Heaven?" Most of the time, I said God and Heaven were in our hearts when we invited Jesus in to be the boss of our lives. He often interpreted that to mean Jesus nestled into a spot in my son's stomach. And this belly understanding led my son to ask us, especially during every holiday season, a barrage of questions about Heaven. The questions elicited quiet, joyful laughter from my husband and me.

"So St. Nick really lived, and he died. So is St. Nicklaus in Heaven?"

"So . . . Santa Claus is in Heaven in my stomach now?"

"If God is real, why can't we see Him?"

Good questions. Hopefully the answers I prayerfully and groggily offered will be of help to him, to myself, to others. Over a decade has passed since my kids were toddlers, and once this essay reaches its final draft my kids will be both almost teens.

Most often as I attempted an answer, a passage from Matthew persistently came to mind: "Whatever you did for one of the least of these brothers [and sisters] of mine, you did for me. . . . Whatever you did not do for one of the least of these, you did not do for me" (Matt. 25:40, 45). That was him! I explain to my son and daughter that caring for the lonely, the hurting or the hungry person is the best way to see Jesus. We also see God in nature, in our parents when they are being kind or wise, and in other people whenever they're taking good care of one another.

Fyodor Dostoevsky thought long and hard about this subject of faith and doubt, during his writing of *The Brothers Karamazov*. He depicted a woman begging a spiritual mentor to help her find faith again. She was aware there might be a God out there somewhere, but she struggled to believe in immortality, the afterlife, or the kindness of God. "I only believed when I was a little child, mechanically, without thinking of anything. How, how is one to prove it? I have come now to lay my soul before you and to ask you about it. If I let this chance slip, no one all my life will answer me. How can I prove it? How can I convince myself?" (Dostoevsky 47).

"There's no proving it, though you can be convinced of it . . . by the experience of active love," answered the wise, old monk. "Strive to love your neighbor actively and indefatigably. Insofar as you advance in love you will grow surer of the reality of God and the immortality of your soul. If you attain to perfect self-forgetfulness in the love of your neighbor, then you will believe without doubt, and no doubt can possibly enter your soul. This has been tried. This is certain" (Dosteovsky 48). Doubts. Many of us struggle to believe not only in God's reality, but in God's *care*.

Resurrecting love.

Resurrecting faith.

When we doubt that God is real, we could set out to really care about the people nearest us. Then we will begin to see God and believe He is good. To counteract doubt, actively love (Dostoevsky, 48).

Like Jesus walking—directly out of a dead man's tomb—with skin on, with breath in his lungs. From the chill and slumber of earth, where his body had spent three dark days, into the open air: where he could again surprise and save women, where he could again reconnect with his standing, unsuspecting comrades, and where he could again fry a real breakfast over the open fire.

Resurrection of love brings a resurrection of our faith. And faith makes a real sound. As audible as my my toddler-twin sisters' laughter finding my ears, finding my heart, when I was four years old.

"So where is Heaven, Mom?"

I don't know, but let's give each other a real hug. The answer will, I believe, soon stand before us, face to face, smiling . . . caring.

SICK KIDS

Sick Kids
Free Verse

Intense cold in North air. I look for virus-free spaces,
while memories chill, from earlier,
those other months, months seeming without end.

Balance lost,
winter or spring cough
within my little ones,
and tense hearts.

Asthma, weak lungs,
bitter draft thru the night,
I become
      tired,
            dazed,
                  crazed.

Watching my son struggle to breathe,
sitting with my son thru the night
near a warm shower
to attain sunrise.

So many activities cancelled,
so many nights wondering,
feeling helpless to stop the coughing,
and week upon week of children's bronchitis,
                  my sleep deprivation.

          I become tired-scared.

Another night sitting with my small son in the bathroom,

                building steam
                to help him breathe. His eyes close, his fever grows.

Then another day, another breath.
A little traumatized, wholly sleep-deprived,

sincere thanks.

Fear

mommy becomes scared

feeling helpless   to help

asthma   plus the cold

inside both of my small children

we want to reach the sunrise

infant coughs every sixty

seconds   wheeze   fading

I look for virus-free air

tense heart from each of these memories

Sick Kids
Heroic Couplet Iambic Pentameter

Haibun

I was so thankful each day we had health.
At times it was summer. Other times: Cough.
At times it was autumn. In spring it—Weeze.

Today a deep virus has taken, sneeze.

There are others who know the sleepless goals.
Mothers who share in this tense heart and fear
ask God or the nurse or someone who hears,
to save these kids: my young heart, my young soul.

Could be a Minnesota winter or a spring
virus in the air, then we didn't stop coughing.
Then, pneumonia. Helping little ones, Mom crazed.
Mom's heart becomes tense, infected. Tired, dazed.

Holding Now:

   a Haibun

Sometimes, it's just plain hard to be joyful on rainy days; this is especially true when we're sleep-deprived. It can be tough to conceive that God is near during cloudy weather. When my first two children were infants, they fought through dozens of viruses, sometimes pneumonia, and my sleep would be sparse and often interrupted. Winters in Minnesota were very long.

In 2013 I participated in a Bible Study about Moses and, through our in-depth look at the Israelites' Exodus across a desert, I came to see clouds as comforting and uplifting nurturers during difficult times. I came to see clouds as God's choice of a lantern, his select mode of encouragement or guidance, his advisor within darkness.

The way was seemingly random, from Egypt to the Promised Land, but the goal was not really the place. The goal was and is God's *presence*. For all of us, He plans that His *presence* is our Promised Land. And it is obedience—no matter how many zig-zag turns He leads us into—obedience even when we feel we're walking in circles. Obedience brings us another step closer to the Promised Land.

                         canaan is waiting while we are traveling

we are israel's

    even i

        adopted into the family of israel

           through Jesus' life, love, death,

                  renewed life

           i am adopted

   Now

into the way of suffering

    woven in from outside of the Torah

           what lucky, chosen people we are

to have Jesus as our brother

God does know our way home
in the desert
Now
the Holy Spirit made manifest

in a pillar of cloud
guide
warmth
guide
eternal designer of this route

God decided
still Now decides
will ever decide
and the closer we israelites get to our promised land
the deeper difficulties we will find
closer to canaan means increasing thirst Now
bleeding feet
losing our way
and with less to eat
fewer sweets

what lucky, chosen people we are.

Now
i am israel's Now

and rescued by a cloud

Free Verse
    We Still Are

the body once was
i saw such energy

then blood like our river

a sudden fall like a clot
i held my child who was not

Works Cited

Dosteovsky, Fyodor. *The Brothers Karamazov*. Edited by Ralph E. Matlaw.
W.W. Norton and Company, Inc., New York, New York, 1976.

Holy Bible. The New International Version Study Bible. Zondervan Publishing House,
1985.

Rutkow, Eric, *American Canopy: Trees, Forests, and the Making of a Nation*.
Scribner, 2013.

Special Thanks

Lukas and Runa, my kids, I thank God for you both. I feel rich, simply being Mom to you.

Linda Lein, thank you for the creative decades and for the whole world of writing! You believed in me, drew forth gifts from me, and called me forward as a writer in each life season. Without you, this book wouldn't have begun, would never have been completed.

Dara Syrkin, thank you for your skillful, editorial eye behind every phrase, every word choice, every tiny piece of punctuation. Your positivity, support, and encouragement have carried me along. Jessica, Kathy, and Sherry, in publishing and design, heartfelt thanks for your expansive expertise and for being on this team.

Inside this marathon of motherhood, along my own road, so many good Samaritans, including all my aunts, have supported me in different ways, on the longer days. A sincere and important thank you to Dad, Gail, Eva, Barb, Diane, Heidi R., Iris, Khanh, Marilyn, MOPS New Brighton, Miriam L., Nancy A., Nancy E., Robyn, and Shelly, for showing up, being a friend, and especially praying for our young family system on the bleaker days. It's not possible to see or recognize all the people who have helped any of us mothers keep going. To everyone on this round earth who, behind the scenes, prays for or cares for young moms, old moms, young dads, or old dads, (or for our marriages), I say thank you. Walter, my handsome husband as well as my literal birthing midwife, thank you for encouraging, expecting, and nudging this book into reality.

Last, and the opposite of least,

thank you to my mom,

for giving galaxies to me, for more than a million eternal gifts,

tak sa myket, for giving me existence.

Reader, you are loved and appreciated. If you've picked up this book then you're likely a weary mother, a weary father, or simply someone who appreciates poetic and philosophical lines of thought. Maybe your soul loves nature and the wilderness as much as mine. Know that I published this memoir-slash-chapbook-slash-volume for your sake.

Perhaps half of these poems, essays, and fiction stories (those not touching on motherhood) were written when I was in my late teens, or experiencing college, or in very early adulthood. You guessed rightly if you had a feeling that the author's voice at times sounded . . . er, youthful? Then the other half of this compilation, the pieces that are indeed mommy-related, were sketched into journals or upon loose scraps of paper whenever I stole a moment for coffee or could secure solid, quiet me-time as a mom. Freelance book-editing for other authors, teaching ESL, and offering piano lessons all kept me pretty busy, too, while forming this book. The teaching, the freelance editing, and the creative writing all served as healthy occasional breaks, from parenting hours or household demands (you already know what that's like).

This collection is indeed a labor of love, involving more than twenty years of working and dreaming, shaping and reshaping, contemplating and rethinking. It was not until my son was in first or second grade that I realized I might honestly move ahead with self-publishing a book like this.

In many ways, this accumulation is a memoir in near-poetry form, a chapbook, an anthology of essays, and a glance back and over my first forty years . . . portraying my take on love, marriage, motherhood, and miscarriage. You may find this is not a book to cruise through, chapter upon chapter. Some days you may need a few minutes mining the last pages, other days you may need a half hour meditating on only the center poems. This collection was never meant to be read only or necessarily from front to back.

Parenthood started for me with a jarring entrance, with a whole lot of ouch—yes, the natural birth was still traumatic even when voluntarily elected, a powerful bronchitis in my own body during those first two weeks with my first child, limited finances (we lived below the state poverty line, felt it was important that I opt to stay home nearly full-time, as my husband worked simultaneously as a part-time graduate student, part-time nursing assistant, and renovator of our fixer-upper first house), and, also stretching: our cross-cultural marriage.

There've been some unique, challenging dynamics and interactions, in our marriage, right from the start. Also, two or three other unseen realities confronting our relationship and our individual selves did impact motherhood, significantly, for me. Yet, this book is whole and complete, even without describing these dynamics or these realities in detail. Good news is that God can and will redeem all of it.

Labor, motherhood, relationship shifts: these are not as intense for some as for others, and I understand that many mothers had much more difficulty than I. Every motherhood or fatherhood encounter is unique. And every miscarriage exists only because a very valuable human being exists, though he or she is not near us to tell their story. Artists, thinkers, parents, anyone in search of God—these poems and prose pieces hold metaphors dear to my heart, resonating with my journey of life. Musicality would have been strangled, and the poems and essays "clunky," had I placed a He/She within each phrase in which I mentioned God. I used only the male pronouns, but I do believe that God is both male and female. Many of the poems have partial punctuation, rather than complete punctuation or zero punctuation. These were all penned on purpose, with care.

I'm praying that these parables, thoughts, and words bring new hope through your winter blues, a new zest into your parenting style, and new light for your next good step. Have a safe trip, around each dark corner.

Your journey is being held and supported, and your pain, too, is so, so rich in meaning.

Forgiveness

Long, long ago and even this morning
watching waters submitted in earthy exhaustion.
Continents collided in stealthy ecstasy.
Even the dominant sun watching from its lofty station
took a startled gasp
as wispy warriors appeared in the foothills
to warn the wounded.
Crazy hatred fumbled backwards one moment,
resisted itself for two moments. No counter-attack.

Why?

Could there be any kinetic glory with
no competition, no conflict? The sun wondered.

Optimism.
This eclipse is like all our other quiet victories:
lonely farm hands will ride their rumbling tractor uphill
into dawn lifting

and fall
into joyful beds of
earthly pearls. Rugged girls
will gaze at the earth so long and so thirstily
they will own it

all.
Entire prisms of ocean rainbows will bend

sadly before the winter's muteness.
Crumbling tiger waves curl with long claws in toward the shore
(waves folding and begging and drinking in the dryness
of subtle sand waiting to eclipse them,
dew-damp, friendly-like).

Hungry, lonely tide will tiptoe in
to find home and acceptance and
a hearty laugh
with an old friend.

Trust the enemy
whom you yourself have empowered.
Kiss the one
who is upheld only by your aching.

Then

    for your own mudded evil,

        and for jagged,

    selfless
            heart-wounds,

       for each ray of unfairness
       you welcomed in too harshly
       via upside-down reflections,

forgive yourself too.